ONLY THE BEST

Steven Saunders

with Graham Hart

ILLUSTRATED BY MARILYN O'NEONS

Photographs by Philip Mynott

O P T I M A

An OPTIMA book

First published in Great Britain in 1993 by Optima,
a division of Little, Brown and Company (UK) Limited.

A CIP catalogue record for this book is
available from the British Library.

Typeset in Sabon by Solidus (Bristol) Limited
Printed and bound in Great Britain by
BPCC Hazell Books Ltd
Member of BPCC Ltd

ISBN 0 356 21013 8

Little, Brown and Company (UK) Limited
165 Great Dover Street
London SE1 4YA

Steven Saunders trained as a chef at London's Savoy hotel. He went on to manage a group of East Anglian hotels, then at the age of 25, he and his wife Sally bought the Pink Geranium Restaurant in the village of Melbourn, near Cambridge. The Pink Geranium has been awarded a Michelin Red M for excellence and has for two years been given two AA rosettes for its high standards of food and service. Steven has had his own food show on BBC Radio Cambridgeshire/Peterborough for five years and also works for the Chiltern Independent radio network as a radio chef. In 1993 he launched a new show on BBC radio called *Dine with Steven*. He writes for various Cambridgeshire/Hertfordshire groups of newspapers as 'food expert' and has a regular weekly page called 'A Fresh Look' in *The Caterer and Hotelkeeper*. In addition to this he has made numerous television appearances.

For Serena and Stefanie with love

CONTENTS

A V next to the recipe indicates that it is suitable for vegetarians or that vegetarian options are included.

Acknowledgements xiv
Introduction xv

1 FIRST FOODS FOR WEANING

Introduction 1
V Baby Carrot, Potato and Orange Purée 4
V Calabrese (Broccoli) and Celeriac Purée with Chives 5
V Swede and Parsnip Purée with Sweet Pimento 6
V Pure Apple Purée 7
V Pear Purée 8
V Banana Purée 9
V Papaya Purée 10
V Carrot and Cauliflower Purée 11
V Spinach Purée 12
V Courgette and Banana Purée 13
V Yellow Lentil and Spinach with Tomato Coulis 14
Free-range, Maize-fed Chicken with Carrots and Fresh Peach 15
Soft Herring Roes with Tomato and Marrow 16
V Gratin Dauphinoise 17
Turkey Breast with Buttered Devon Swedes 18
V Cauliflower and Courgette au gratin 19
Avocado Mousse 20
V Cucumber Cheese Mousse 21
V Sole and Prawn Mousse 22
V Banana Milkshake 23

2 BREAKFASTS

Introduction 24
Ⅴ Wheat Biscuits with Banana Mash 25
Banana and Bacon Rolls 26
Ⅴ Exotic Fruit Muesli 27
Ⅴ Orangey Apples and Banana 28
Ⅴ Crêpes – the Basic Mix 29
Ⅴ Crêpes with Fruit Fillings 30
Ⅴ Scottish Pancakes 31
Ⅴ Crêpes with Scrambled Eggs and Smoked Salmon 32
Liver Casserole 33
Ⅴ Honey Muesli Munch 34
Face Breakfast 35
Ⅴ Steven's Yoghurt 36
Ⅴ Porridge Oats with Banana and Mango 37
Ⅴ Muffins with Mushrooms, Beef Tomatoes and Cheddar Cheese flavoured with Tarragon 38
Ⅴ Baskets of Scrambled Egg 39
Ⅴ Porridge Cookies 40
Ⅴ Dried Fruit Spread 41
Ⅴ Fromage Frais Fruit Spread 42

3 JUST A QUICK SNACK

Introduction 43
Ⅴ Finger Foods (some ideas) 44
Ⅴ Finger Pitta Breads 45
Ⅴ Turkish Hummus 46
Oriental Style Chicken 47
Surprise Meatballs 48
Chicken Parfaït 49
Salmon Muffins 50
Danish Fritters 51
Ⅴ Saté Bread 52
Ⅴ Tarragon Eggs 'En Cocotte' 53

Ⅴ Traditional Welsh Rarebit   54
Ⅴ Fresh Herb Melba Toast   55

4   STOCKS, SOUPS AND SAUCES

Introduction   56
Ⅴ Vegetable Stock   58
Light Chicken Stock   59
Light Fish Stock   60
Avocado and Prawn Soup   61
Ⅴ Cream of Fresh Tomato and Basil Soup   62
Ⅴ 'Petits-Pois' Soup   63
Ⅴ Creamy Carrot and Celeriac Soup   64
Ⅴ Cauliflower and Cheese Soup   65
Ⅴ Spinach, Orange and Nutmeg Soup   66
Ⅴ Wild Mushroom Soup with Tarragon   67
Smoked Haddock Chowder   68
Ⅴ Country Vegetable Soup   69
Ⅴ Green Lentil Soup   70
Ⅴ Leek and Potato Soup   71
Ⅴ Simple Tomato Soup/Sauce   72
Ⅴ Beurre Blanc Scented with Celery   73

5   FISH DISHES

Introduction   74
Goujons of Sole with a Fennel Sauce   75
Fillets of Sole with Grapes Veronique   76
Flakes of Salmon with Chive Sauce   77
Salmon Mousse with Sauce Provençale   78
Creamy Soft Roes with Mushrooms   79
Garlic Monkfish   80
Salmon Mornay   81
Sole Florentine   82
Cod Fillet with Dill and Basil   83

Plaice with Duxelle Filling   84
Parisienne of Smoked Haddock with Tomato Coulis   86
Savoy Kedgeree   87
Family Fish Pie   88
Yoghurt Quiche with Tuna Fish   89
Homemade Fish Cakes   90

6 MAIN DISHES (NON VEGETARIAN)

Introduction   91
𝒱 Pasta (for noodles)   93
Fricassée of Maize-fed Chicken with Basil Flavoured Tagliatelle   94
Lambs' Liver Casserole   95
Wholewheat Pasta and Tuna Fish Casserole   96
Goujons of Turkey Fillet with a Garlic Crust   97
Guinea Fowl with Banana Casserole Scented with Tarragon   98
Escalope of Turkey Breast 'Fines Herbs'   100
Citrus Chicken   101
Breast of Pheasant with Citrus Sauce   102
Lambs' Kidney 'Oriental'   103
Ragoût of Beef (Normandy)   104
Spicy Spaghetti (Milligetti)   105
Veggie Bake   106
Casserole of Beef and Vegetables with a Shallot Sauce   107
Calves' Liver with Fresh Sage and Caramelized Onions   108
Lamb Tikka Kebabs   109
Beef and Coriander Sausages   110

7 MAIN MEALS (VEGETARIAN)

Introduction   111
𝒱 Lentil Shepherd's Pie   112
𝒱 Vegetable Gratin   114
𝒱 Oriental Spinach   115
𝒱 Carrot Mousseline (Encased in Leek Leaves)   116

Ⅴ Baby Broad Beans with Parsley and Lemon   118
Ⅴ Fromage Frais Bakers   119
Ⅴ Fresh Beans on Toast   120
Ⅴ Cassata   121
Ⅴ Creamy Mushrooms   122
Ⅴ Spicy Cheese and Tomato Dip   123
Ⅴ Pasta with Pesto Sauce   124
Ⅴ Ratatouille (with Brown Rice)   125
Ⅴ Spanish Omelette   126
Ⅴ Vegetable Rissoles   128
Ⅴ Baked Bean Burger   129
Ⅴ Baked Bean Pie   130
Ⅴ Fricassée of Eggs with Tarragon   131
Ⅴ Cheese and Hazelnut Hot Pot   132
Ⅴ Baby Rice and Vegetables   133

8 SWEET DREAMS

Introduction   134
Ⅴ Pineapple Prizes   135
Ⅴ Coconut Ice-cream with Mango Coulis   136
Ⅴ Simple Chocolate Mousse   138
Ⅴ Banana Clouds   139
Ⅴ Steven's Special Chocolate Tart   140
Ⅴ Carrot Cake   141
Ⅴ Traditional Fruit Cake (for Birthdays. etc.)   143
Ⅴ Real Blancmange   144
Ⅴ Honey Fool   145
Ⅴ Strawberry Syllabub   146
Ⅴ Cottage Cheese and Fruit Mousse   147
Ⅴ Fresh Pineapple Cheesecake   148
Ⅴ Baked Custard with Nutmeg   150
Ⅴ Yoghurt Scones   151
Ⅴ Peach Scone   152
Ⅴ Syrup Scones   153
Ⅴ Upside-down Currant Buns   154

Ⅴ Date and Honey Bars   155
Ⅴ Peanut Butter Cookies   156
Ⅴ Banana Cake   157
Ⅴ Banana Brownies   158
Ⅴ Gingerbread Men   159
Ⅴ Fresh Raspberry Jelly   160
Ⅴ Yoghurt Fool   161
Ⅴ Summer Pudding   162
Ⅴ Fruit Coulis (Purées)   163
Ⅴ Passion Fruit Coulis   163
Ⅴ Vanilla Custard   164

9 PARTY TIME

Introduction   165
Chicken, Onion and Sweetcorn Potato Cakes   166
Barbecued Spicy Chicken Drumsticks   167
Ⅴ Cottage Cheese Dip   168
Ⅴ Cheese Straws with Tomato   169
Treasure Purses   170
Ⅴ Wiggly Worm Cheese Pastries   172
Bacon and Sweetcorn Fritters   173
Ⅴ Pitta Bread Pockets   174
Ⅴ Mini Pizzas   175
Ⅴ Egg Heads   176
Ⅴ Rice Crispie Savouries   177
Ⅴ Mexican Dip   178
Devil Dogs   179
Ⅴ Orangesnap Baskets   180
Ⅴ Space People   182
Scrummy Snails   184
Ⅴ Hedgehogs and Ladybirds   185
Viking Ships   186
Ⅴ Watermelon Boats   187
Ⅴ Knickerbocker Glory   188
Ⅴ Birthday Cake – Basic Sponge Recipe   189

10 PICNICS AND PACKED LUNCHES

Introduction   190
Sandwiches – some new ideas   191
Kipper Paté   193
Chicken Liver Paté   194
Ⅴ Catherine Wheel Sandwiches   195
Ⅴ Serena's Carrot Salad   196
Ⅴ Cheesy Pasties   197
Ⅴ Picnic Squares   198
Sardine Tart   199
Cornish Pasties   200
Scottish Cheesemeats   202
Ⅴ Wholemeal Tomato Quiche   203
Ⅴ Apple Cake   204
Ⅴ Stuffed Tomatoes with Tuna   205
Ⅴ Rice Crispie Balls   206
Ⅴ Fast Food Pizzas   207

All amounts are in imperial and metric. The latter are
approximations, either rounded up or rounded down.

The following abbreviations have been used for oven settings:

A – Gas mark 2/3 or Electricity 150°/160°C
B – Gas mark 5 or Electricity 190°C
C – Gas mark 8 or Electricity 230°C

Acknowledgements

There are two main reasons I consider this book to be special. One is because it is dedicated to my two lovely girls, Serena and Stefanie, and the second is because it is my first ever book published.

I hope to be able to publish many more books on my subject of 'food' but couldn't have written this one without the help and knowledge of my wife Sally, who has 'reared' our children.

I would also like to thank Graham Hart for all his hard work in compiling some of my very unreadable recipes and 'memoirs' into a most readable, interesting and enjoyable book!

In my opinion it is the combination of all of our knowledge and talents that sets this book apart from others.

I would also like to acknowledge my mother, Joy Saunders, for it was her idea to write this book in the first place!

Finally I would like to thank my publisher, Hilary Foakes, who has been tremendously patient (with all the various complications we have encountered) and remained true to her word and published *Only the Best*!

INTRODUCTION

It seems like all of my life I have spent learning, writing, broadcasting and appreciating food. It has always been a subject very close to my heart. When my first child arrived (Serena) she made me a very proud father and, like any proud parent, I wanted only the best of everything for her. At the time of her birth, commercial baby foods were having a rough time. Jars of food were being sabotaged with glass and the Food Commission decided that as many as 40 per cent of commercial baby foods failed to provide the nutrient levels recommended. I didn't hesitate therefore to start compiling some ideas to provide my child with some of the fresh, pure foods that we have become accustomed to in our restaurant. There really is no replacement for the real thing! Fresh natural foods, free of preservatives, additives and colourings, are the best choice.

Serena has now grown up to be an extremely healthy, attractive and lively four-year-old girl. Her eyes sparkle and her long hair shines – she is a picture of health. My other child, Stefanie, (aged sixteen months) is also gorgeous. She too has long, shiny hair and a lively personality. I know that their diet has had a lot to do with the way they are now – they are living proof of the success that fresh, homegrown, quality food can achieve.

I have written this book so that you too can share some of my natural, unadulterated recipes. (I've used the feminine pronoun throughout the book, but I can assure you that boys will enjoy the food just as much as my girls.) Both Serena and Stefanie now refuse to eat processed and convenience foods like burgers and fish fingers – they actually turn their noses up and say 'Where's Daddy's food, I want Daddy's food!'

So here it is – a sort of 'gourmet food book for children' – 'Daddy's Food' in print – at last!

STEVEN SAUNDERS

1
FIRST FOODS FOR WEANING

INTRODUCTION

F eeding a baby solid foods for the first time can cause parents a great deal of anxiety. Like many aspects of baby-care, there's plenty of free advice given: you *should* do this, you *must* not do that! In general, however, it's not essential to be an expert in either cookery or nutrition. The most important requirement is a good measure of common sense. As long as you remember that your baby needs to eat foods that contain the essential vitamins, proteins and minerals, you cannot go far wrong. Your health visitor or a good child-care book will tell you which these essential nutrients are.

Sally and I started giving our children, Serena and Stefanie, solid foods at only three to four months. But they were the times that suited our children. You must do what you think is best for your own. Have a chat with your health visitor if you're not sure. At that point both of ours started crying after having been fed by Sally and it seemed obvious that they needed more than mother's milk to keep them happy. It was then that we began weaning – the changeover from milk to solid foods.

A WEANING GUIDE

Here are a few simple guidelines, but if in doubt, consult your doctor.

- During weaning, do not forget that milk is still the major part of your baby's diet. You can mix solid foods and milk by offering them both at the same feed, with the solid food coming either before or after the milk.

- As your baby gets to cope with and enjoy small tastes of solid food, start experimenting by introducing a variety of ingredients.

- Always remember that a baby needs plenty of liquid. Previously boiled water or well-diluted fresh fruit juice can be provided in addition to the normal amounts of milk.

- By about six months, solid foods will be a major part of your baby's diet. Now is the time to introduce different textures to her food ... while still keeping up the supply of milk (about one pint per day). Don't worry, though, if your child stops drinking milk after coming off the breast, as occasionally happens; just make sure she gets plenty of calcium from elsewhere e.g. cheese, yoghurts, white bread, sesame seeds, etc.

- As your baby grows a little you can give her foods to hold. Some of the finger foods in Chapter 3 are ideal for this. With young babies, however, always keep a careful watch on them while eating, in case of choking.

MEALS FOR WEANING

All the meals in this chapter recommend the use of a food processor or blender to produce purées. But while such a piece of equipment is clearly a great advantage, it is not essential. You can use the back of a spoon to force the ingredients through a sieve to give excellent results ... only it takes a little longer.

You may find that you can't process some foods finely enough and a sieve may be useful in ensuring that purées are smooth enough for very young children. Whatever you use, you'll soon discover how best to purée your ingredients. And you'll quickly learn that it's best to make too much rather than too little – children do tend to spill a lot.

When cooking vegetables for purées, especially those for the very young, you need to boil them for longer than normal. Whereas you might normally cook *al dente*, or 'to the bite', you need to cook until soft for use in a purée. The times given in the methods are all approximate; keep an eye on the vegetables until they're ready. Never let them cook so long that they change colour or start to mush in the pan. And keep a lid on the pan while cooking to retain the vitamins.

I recommend the use of small, baby vegetables if they are available, but they are difficult to get sometimes. They are sweeter, easier and quicker to cook. A last point about cooking vegetables is to remember always to save the stock. It will contain some of the goodness of the vegetables and may be useful for diluting or moistening the purée later, during the preparation of the dish.

When serving meals, check to see that the food is luke warm throughout. Food left for a few moments in a processor may cool near the top but still be very hot in the middle. Always serve the food fresh. Apart from retaining the taste, you will have fewer worries about hygiene if you cut down on re-heating and storing. For these reasons I don't really like the specially manufactured baby dishes that keep food warm, although I accept they may be useful at times.

And finally, remember to try out ideas of your own. There are only a handful of recipes in this chapter, but hundreds of variations can be derived from these. You can utilize small amounts of foods left over after preparing your own meals. And with one of the new hand-held portable food processors you can produce instant meals from what you have been served in other people's homes. Why not? If you consider the food to be good enough for your baby then it is a great compliment to your host.

BABY CARROT, POTATO AND ORANGE PURÉE

Age	3 months upwards
Preparation time	10 minutes
Cooking time	10 minutes
Serves	1

Purées don't have to be boring.
Think about possible combinations of ingredients. This one is made
more interesting by the addition of the orange, although you can experiment with other
vegetables as well as fruits.

INGREDIENTS

*3–4 baby carrots (or a small
    regular carrot)*
1 small potato
1 small orange

METHOD

1. Peel the carrot(s) and slice into inch pieces.
2. Prepare the potato in the same way.
3. Cut the orange in half; peel one half and be careful to remove all the pips and pith.
4. Boil 2 inches of water in a saucepan, simmer the vegetables with half the orange for 10 minutes.
5. Drain and process in a blender until smooth.
6. Add the juice from the other half of the orange to flavour, and serve while luke warm.

TIP

A whole orange may make this a little acidic. Use your judgement, and your baby's tastes, to decide on amounts. You could also use a sweet potato and omit both the potato and the orange ... with fresh, simple ingredients, you can't go far wrong.

CALABRESE (BROCCOLI) AND CELERIAC PURÉE WITH CHIVES

Age	3 months upwards
Preparation time	10 minutes
Cooking time	20 minutes
Serves	1

Calabrese (sometimes better known as broccoli) is a delicious vegetable and is very high in iron. However, it's important not to cook it into a purée before you process it. Overcooking, especially with young, tender florets will kill all the natural goodness. Celeriac is also a very tasty vegetable. If you're not familiar with it, it is a rather ugly, brown and white, knobbly root vegetable, with a celery-like flavour, that cooks like a swede.

INGREDIENTS

2 florets of calabrese (or broccoli)
1 heaped tablespoon of chopped celeriac (¹/₂ inch cubes)
unsalted butter
chives

METHOD

1. Wash the calabrese and celeriac; chop the celeriac into ¹/₂ inch cubes. Finely chop about 6 stalks of fresh chives.
2. Boil the celeriac in 2 inches of water for 10 minutes.
3. After 10 minutes add the calabrese florets and cook for a further 7 minutes.
4. Drain, and add the chives and a knob of unsalted butter.
5. Blend into a smooth purée and serve luke warm.

TIP

Celeriac is a large vegetable – but this recipe only requires a small amount. Plan your own meals so you can use the celeriac in another meal at the same time.

SWEDE AND PARSNIP PURÉE WITH SWEET PIMENTO

Age	3 months upwards
Preparation time	10 minutes
Cooking time	20 minutes
Serves	1

Pimento, or pepper, is very high in vitamin C and, if used carefully, gives a variety to the flavour of foods that babies will love. Use the pimento sparingly at first until your baby acquires a taste for it, or not!

INGREDIENTS

1 small swede
I small parsnip
½ small red pimento (pepper)

METHOD

1. Peel both the swede and the parsnip and cut into ½ inch cubes.
2. Wash the piece of pepper, cut in half and remove any stalk, seeds and pith. Cube into ½ inch pieces.
3. Boil parsnips and swede for 15 minutes.
4. Add the pepper to the boiling vegetables and cook for a further 5 minutes.
5. Drain, process until smooth and serve luke warm.

TIP

With ingredients like swede and parsnip it is important to use fresh, young vegetables. The taste, and the textures, of older swedes and parsnips may be too strong for very young children.

PURE APPLE PURÉE

Age	3 months upwards
Preparation time	2 minutes
Cooking time	10 minutes
Serves	2

INGREDIENTS

2 medium-sized eating apples

METHOD

1. Peel, halve, core and slice the apples.
2. Place in a saucepan with enough water to cover and cook over a low heat for 10 minutes until soft.
3. Purée the mixture in a blender.

TIP

You can add a little sugar to the water if the apples are sharp to the taste. A stick of cinnamon added to the apples during cooking will produce a slightly different but delicious flavour, but do remember to remove the stick before puréeing.

PEAR PURÉE

Age	3 months upwards
Preparation time	2 minutes
Cooking time	8 minutes
Serves	2

INGREDIENTS

2 ripe pears

METHOD

1. Peel, halve and core the pears and cut into small pieces.
2. Cover with a little water and cook for 8 minutes over a low heat until soft.
3. Purée the mixture.

TIP

Conference pears seem to cook to purée best of all. This purée can be used to slightly sweeten up a savoury purée when baby needs some extra encouragement to eat it!

BANANA PURÉE

Age	3 months upwards
Preparation time	2 minutes
Cooking time	none
Serves	1

INGREDIENTS

1 very ripe banana
a little milk

METHOD

1. Boil a little milk and pour over the peeled banana, mashing with a fork. Serve on its own or with various cereals such as wheat biscuits.

TIP

If you don't have a banana ripe enough, you can split the skin and heat it in the oven or microwave for a couple of minutes to soften before preparing.

Papaya Purée

Age	3 months upwards
Preparation time	2 minutes
Cooking time	3–5 minutes
Serves	1

INGREDIENTS

1 medium-sized papaya

METHOD

1. Cut the fruit in half, remove all the black seeds and scoop out the flesh.
2. Steam for 3–5 minutes, then purée.

TIP

Instead of steaming, you can poach the papaya in a little water to soften, if you wish.

CARROT AND CAULIFLOWER PURÉE

Age	3 months upwards
Preparation time	5 minutes
Cooking time	20 minutes
Serves	2

INGREDIENTS

2 oz (50g) carrots
6 oz (175g) cauliflower florets
2 tablespoons baby milk

METHOD

1. Scrape and slice the carrots and boil for 10 minutes.
2. Then, wash and dry the cauliflower and add to the carrots.
3. Continue to boil the vegetables for a further 5–10 minutes until soft.
4. Drain, and purée in a processor. Stir in 2 tablespoons of baby milk.

TIP

Add a few chopped herbs: such as chives, dill, tarragon and basil for increased flavour.

SPINACH PURÉE

Age	3 months upwards
Preparation time	10 minutes
Cooking time	3 minutes
Serves	2

INGREDIENTS

4 oz (100g) spinach leaves

METHOD

1. Wash the spinach leaves very carefully, removing the coarse stalks and gritty dirt. Immerse in boiling water and simmer with the pan lid on for about 3 minutes.
2. Firmly press out all the excess cooking water and blend the spinach in a processor to purée.

TIP

You can add a little cream (once processed) to soften it, but if you are intending to keep it in the fridge for a few days then omit this.

COURGETTE AND BANANA PURÉE

Age	3 months upwards
Preparation time	8 minutes
Cooking time	5 minutes
Serves	2

INGREDIENTS

1 small courgette
½ small banana

METHOD

1. Wash, trim and slice the courgette and then steam or poach for 5 minutes.
2. Peel and slice the banana and purée together with the courgette.

TIP

Various other vegetables can be added to banana for interesting and complementary flavours: such as swede, parsnip, spinach or carrot.

YELLOW LENTIL AND SPINACH WITH TOMATO COULIS

Age	3 months upwards
Preparation time	15 minutes
Cooking time	25–45 minutes
Serves	1

A coulis is a very fine purée. To achieve the best results in making a coulis
you need to use an extra fine sieve. This particular recipe, because it involves lentils, takes
a little more planning than some of the other more 'instant' purées.

INGREDIENTS

4 leaves of fresh spinach
2 tablespoons of yellow or green
*   lentils*
2 whole tomatoes

METHOD

1. *Either* soak the lentils overnight in cold water, and boil until soft (about 20 minutes);
   Or wash thoroughly and boil in a covered pan for about 40 minutes.
2. Wash the spinach leaves thoroughly and remove any coarse stalks. Chop roughly and boil in $1/2$ inch of pre-boiling water for 5 minutes.
3. Peel the tomatoes and purée them through a fine sieve into a clean bowl.
4. Blend the lentils and spinach together and gently warm the tomato coulis.
5. Serve the vegetable purée with the tomato coulis; both should be luke warm.

TIP

When using lentils it is better to soak them overnight if you can remember to do so. Put them in a large bowl with plenty of cold water and cover the bowl. Room temperature or below is fine, but there's no need to refrigerate.

FREE-RANGE, MAIZE-FED CHICKEN WITH CARROTS AND FRESH PEACH

Age	3 months upwards
Preparation time	15 minutes
Cooking time	5 minutes
Serves	1

This is not so much a recipe,
more a recommendation for a good combination of tastes. I am not suggesting
you cook your chicken especially, but use a small off-cut from a chicken you have cooked
for yourself.

INGREDIENTS

½ breast of free-range, maize-fed
  chicken (pre-roasted)
1 small carrot
1 small fresh peach

METHOD

1. Prepare a purée of carrot and peach as you would the carrot, potato and orange purée on page 4 – just leave out the potato – and, as before, save half the peach juice.
2. Remove any skin from your chicken, slice finely and re-heat thoroughly.
3. Add the chicken to the purée and blend again.
4. Add the remaining juice from the peach and process for a minute or two more. Serve luke warm.

TIP

Free-range, maize-fed chickens have a superior flavour in my opinion. They are also more expensive . . . but worth it. Fresh peach is my favourite to go with this dish, but if you can't get hold of one you can use banana, orange or another fruit of your choice.

SOFT HERRING ROES WITH TOMATO AND MARROW

Age	3 months upwards
Preparation time	10 minutes
Cooking time	15 minutes
Serves	1

Sometimes children's meals are not very appealing to adults. The combination of the herring roes with the vegetables may be a little unexpected, but it is simply delicious. Make some for yourself as well as your children and try it. You may be surprised!

INGREDIENTS

1 oz (25g) of soft herring roes
(tinned or fresh)
1 tomato
½ small marrow
a little cow's milk

METHOD

1. Peel and chop the marrow into ½ inch cubes.
2. Boil the roes in a little cow's milk for 3 minutes.
3. Peel, chop and de-seed the tomatoes and add to the roe.
4. Cook for a further 2 minutes; set aside and allow to cool.
5. Add the marrow to about 1 inch of boiling water and cook for about 7 minutes.
6. Add the marrow to the tomato and roe; blend together and serve luke warm.

TIP

You can add about a ½ teaspoon of Marmite to this for extra flavour, but not too much because Marmite has a high salt content. Salt, added in very small quantities from time to time, is not a problem.

GRATIN DAUPHINOISE

Age	3 months upwards
Preparation time	15 minutes
Cooking time	40 minutes
Serves	1

You could say that Gratin Dauphinoise is the posh name for 'cheesy potato'. It makes a delicious dish on its own but, of course, you can always add other foods to it: like avocado, vegetable purées, fish or minced meat. I have suggested milk in my list of ingredients but you could use half cream and half milk.

INGREDIENTS

1 small potato
1 small onion or shallot
½ pint (300ml) milk
1 oz (25g) mild Cheddar cheese.

METHOD

1. Scrub, peel and thinly slice the potatoes and onions.
2. Arrange these in layers in a small baking tray or dish.
3. Bring the milk to the boil in a saucepan and pour over the potatoes and onions.
4. Grate the cheese and sprinkle this liberally over the other ingredients.
5. Bake in a medium preheated oven for about 35 minutes or until golden brown.
6. Mash it with the back of a fork (or purée through a sieve) and serve luke warm.

TIP

Slice the potato as finely as possible to ensure that it cooks through thoroughly. If you feel adventurous, you can add a little (but only a little!) fresh pimento to give it a delicious flavour.

TURKEY BREAST WITH BUTTERED DEVON SWEDES

Age	3 months upwards
Preparation time	15 minutes
Cooking time	15 minutes
Serves	1

Turkey makes a change from chicken for children and adults alike. The banana makes these more savoury dishes easier to eat for young children. Actually it's quite delicious!

INGREDIENTS

1 small swede
1 small escalope of turkey,
  weighing approx. 4 oz (100g)
½ banana
a little cow's milk
unsalted butter

METHOD

1. Peel the swede and cut into ½ inch cubes; boil for about 15 minutes in a little water with a large knob of unsalted butter.
2. Remove any skin from the turkey breast, slice finely into strips and fry in unsalted butter until thoroughly cooked.
3. Slice the banana and combine all of the ingredients in a food processor with about 1 tablespoonful of milk.
4. Process until smooth and serve luke warm.

TIP

I always think it is a good idea to add something that is naturally sweet to a savoury dish for children. It seems to make the difference between success and failure. If your child blatantly refuses her dinner (it has been known in the Saunders' household), try adding some fruit yoghurt, fromage frais or fresh fruits to the dish.

CAULIFLOWER AND COURGETTE AU GRATIN

Age	3 months upwards
Preparation time	10 minutes
Cooking time	15 minutes
Serves	1

Something that is *au gratin* should be glazed with cheese,
so this recipe title is slightly inaccurate. It does, however, sound better
than 'mixed with melted cheese', which is what we are doing. The florets of fresh, young
cauliflower are good to eat raw in salads, but not for new babies. They
need a reasonable amount of cooking to make them suitable for the very young.

INGREDIENTS

2 florets of cauliflower
1 baby courgette or
    ½ normal-sized courgette
1 dessertspoon of grated, mild,
    Cheddar cheese

METHOD

1. Wash the cauliflower florets and peel and thinly slice the courgettes.
2. Boil the cauliflower in 2 inches of water for 10 minutes.
3. After the 10 minutes, add the thinly sliced courgettes and cook together for a further 5 minutes.
4. Drain and process in a blender until smooth.
5. Add the grated cheese, blend in and serve luke warm.

TIP

With young cauliflower you can use the stalk of the florets, but not if the vegetable is slightly older as they will be tough.

AVOCADO MOUSSE

Age	6 months upwards
Preparation time	25 minutes
Cooking time	none
Serves	4

This is an excellent recipe when you have the time, and will keep in the refrigerator for up to 4–5 days. It can be used as a snack before meals, perhaps with toast.

INGREDIENTS

¹/₂ oz (15g) gelatine
¹/₄ pint (150ml) chicken or
    vegetable stock
2 large or 3 small avocados
¹/₂ large onion
¹/₄ pint (150ml) mayonnaise
¹/₄ pint (150ml) fresh double cream
salt
freshly ground pepper
juice of one lemon
Worcestershire sauce

METHOD

1. Dissolve the gelatine in a bowl by sprinkling it over about ¹/₄ pint of warm water; keep this warm by placing the bowl over a saucepan of hot water.
2. Stir in the stock and allow to cool.
3. Mash the avocados with the lemon juice until smooth, having taken care to remove all the skin, stone and pith.
4. Grate the onion finely until you have about 1 teaspoonful of paste; add this to the avocado, and season with salt, pepper and Worcestershire sauce. Add the lemon juice.
5. Slowly pour the gelatine mixture into this and stir until it is just beginning to thicken.
6. Whip the cream until it is slightly stiffened, but still soft, and mix it and the mayonnaise into the avocado mixture.
7. Pour the mixture into a large mould and chill until firm.
8. You can cover the top of the mousse with more lemon juice and cling film to keep it very fresh for up to 4–5 days.

TIP

Make sure the mould is buttered first, before introducing the mousse into it. You will notice the difference when you turn it out.

CUCUMBER CHEESE MOUSSE

Age	1 year upwards
Preparation time	30 minutes
Cooking time	none
Serves	4

This is another tasty and easy to prepare mousse. It requires no cooking,
just a little heating of water, and keeps well (up to a week in an airtight container) in a
refrigerator. It has a multitude of uses, such as in sandwiches or with
toast, although my family enjoy it best when accompanying fish or meat.

INGREDIENTS

1 cucumber
8 oz (225g) full-fat soft cheese
¼ pint (150ml) mayonnaise
½ oz (15g) gelatine
¼ pint (150ml) of water
½ level teaspoon salt
2 level teaspoons castor sugar
salt
¼ pint (150ml) fresh double cream

METHOD

1. Remove the skin and seeds from the cucumber and chop the flesh.
2. Blend the cheese until soft and combine with the mayonnaise.
3. Dissolve the gelatine by sprinkling it over about ¼ pint of warm water. Keep this warm by placing the bowl over a saucepan of hot water. Add the castor sugar and a dash of salt. Allow this to cool.
4. Whisk the fresh cream until it is softly stiff and then combine all the ingredients together – finally adding in the cucumber.
5. This mixture needs thorough stirring, until it forms a thick creamy paste that can be poured or spooned into a large mould.
6. Keep the mousse cool until just before turning out.

TIP
You can add a little lemon or lime juice to this, which will give it both a tasty tang and help preserve it.

SOLE AND PRAWN MOUSSE

Age	6 months upwards
Preparation time	15 minutes
Cooking time	40–45 minutes
Serves	4/6

My two children always seem to like the foods that cost the most to prepare. This one, therefore, is a particular favourite, as you can probably guess by looking at the list of ingredients. You can, of course, make it without the prawns and you can also reduce the cost further by mixing the sole with another fish such as plaice or haddock.

INGREDIENTS

1 lb (450g) fillets of sole
2 oz (50g) shelled prawns
1 egg white
3 egg yolks
salt
white pepper
¼ pint (450ml) fresh double cream
3 oz (75g) unsalted butter
lemon juice
tomato purée

METHOD

1. Skin and chop the sole and combine this with the shelled prawns, egg white, a dash of salt and about ¼ level teaspoonful of white pepper.
2. Purée this mixture in a blender with about ⅔ of the available cream. Remember to keep the proportions equal if you are unable to purée the entire mixture in one go.
3. Using individual ovenproof ramekins if you can (if not, use small overproof bowls of any suitable shape), press the mixture well down into the dishes and stand in a refrigerator for about 3 hours.
4. After this period, cook in the oven in a water bath at a low heat (A) for 35 minutes. Turn out to drain and keep them warm.
5. In a bowl over a pan of hot water, combine the egg yolks, a knob of butter and a teaspoonful of lemon juice. Stir this until the mixture is running but with a creamy 'coating' consistency.

6. Remove from the heat and slowly beat in the rest of the butter and about a teaspoonful of tomato purée. Having whipped the remaining fresh cream until softly stiff, fold this into the sauce and return it to the heat to thicken; do not boil, and keep stirring gently.

7. When the sauce is ready, place the mousselines on a warmed plate and pour the sauce around them. Serve hot.

TIP
A last word on costs . . . don't buy best Dover sole if it's too expensive – use lemon sole fillets.

BANANA MILKSHAKE

Age	4 months upwards
Preparation time	10 minutes
Cooking time	none
Serves	4

This is a refreshing and nutritious drink,
ideally served chilled – give it to your children on a hot day!

INGREDIENTS

1 pint (575ml) cool, fresh milk
2–3 level tablespoons drinking chocolate
5 oz (140g) natural yoghurt
2 bananas

METHOD

1. Liquidize all the ingredients in a food processor until smooth.
2. Chill four glasses and pour in the mixture.

2
BREAKFASTS

INTRODUCTION

When I have talked to friends about my ideas for children's food they have sometimes held up their hands in horror, asking just how parents can expect to find the time to prepare some of the dishes I recommend. The 'no time' argument applies particularly to breakfast, when most modern parents seem to be in a desperate hurry. The same parents, however, will agree that breakfast is an important meal, especially for young children. So, somewhere a compromise has to be found between supplying a nourishing meal for your child and not spending too much time preparing it.

I hope I have got the balance about right with my suggestions, combining excellent food, full of natural goodness, with quick and easy preparation. Take the first recipe in this section for example: it consists of a cereal you probably have in your cupboard, a little milk and half a banana ... it couldn't be easier, yet it constitutes a healthy and tasty breakfast that is just a little different from normal. Preparation time? About 2 minutes!

Of course milk is a very useful source of vitamins and protein, so many of the recipes use it. More than some other nationalities, the British tend to think of milk as a breakfast drink or cereal accompaniment. I recommend full-fat cow's milk for children under four years for its taste and goodness, and soya milk for children allergic to dairy products.

You don't have to be tied to traditional thinking, however, and I hope I have given a few suggestions for foods which you might not associate with breakfast time. Providing a dish is part of a diet that is balanced over the whole day, it doesn't really matter what the child eats, providing she enjoys it and it provides the right nourishment.

Finally it's worth making a point about a good old standby that I haven't listed as a separate meal ... and that is toast. Toast is much underrated, but when made with good bread and nutritious toppings, perhaps bananas, or honey, or Marmite, it can become a very important part of a child's daily diet.

WHEAT BISCUITS WITH BANANA MASH

Age	6 months upwards
Preparation time	2 minutes
Cooking time	3 minutes
Serves	1

When I say 'wheat biscuits' I am thinking of Weetabix –
but today several supermarket chains produce their own brands that
go under a variety of names. This old favourite recipe of mine is one that set me thinking
about 'better' food for children. It's so easy to make and is full of goodness.
I have yet to find a child who doesn't like this recipe.

INGREDIENTS

1 wheat biscuit
½ banana
2 fl oz (60ml) cow's milk.

METHOD

1. Boil the milk and pour it on top of the wheat biscuits until soft and mushy.
2. Add the banana and mash it down with a fork until well blended into the mush!

TIP

I particularly recommend this dish because the banana sweetens the Weetabix and avoids the need for sugar. Sugar can be harmful to a baby's teeth and/or gums, amongst other things, and has very limited nutritional value. I try to avoid using it altogether in a young person's diet as it also prevents them developing a sweet tooth. Apart from that, the dish tastes scrummy without sugar.

BANANA AND BACON ROLLS

Age	2–4 years
Preparation time	10 minutes
Cooking time	3–4 minutes
Serves	1

Bananas were a great favourite
when both Serena and Stefanie were very young, and they still love them
today. This dish was particularly popular – a lovely combination of crispy bacon and soft,
sweet bananas.

INGREDIENTS

1 small banana
2 rashers back bacon

METHOD

1. Cut the banana into 4 or 5 small pieces.
2. First derind the bacon; then lay the rashers on a chopping board and 'bat' out with a rolling pin to make them as thin as possible.
3. Wrap each piece of banana up in the lean bacon and cut to size. Secure with a cocktail stick.
4. Cook under a hot grill for 3–4 minutes each side and serve warm.

TIP

Bacon can be salty, especially when smoked. I have no qualms about recommending this dish, but I wouldn't serve it too often. Unsmoked bacon, naturally, lessens the saltiness.

EXOTIC FRUIT MUESLI

Age	1 year upwards
Preparation time	10 minutes
Cooking time	none
Serves	2

Since both muesli and fruit are good sources
of fibre, this recipe makes both a tasty and healthy combination. I know
that the recommended five fruits make an excellent combination, but you can experiment
and adapt. Mixing a few citrus and non-citrus fruits helps, as does the
addition of the banana as a sweetener.

INGREDIENTS

2 tablespoons muesli
1/2 mango
1/2 peach
2 or 3 thin slices of banana
1/2 dozen seedless grapes (skinned)
1/2 apple
1 tablespoon plain, low-fat yoghurt
a little cow's milk

METHOD

1. Wash, peel and chop the fresh fruits into small pieces.
2. Mix the muesli and yoghurt in a bowl.
3. Blend well together with a little milk to help the consistency.

TIP

When selecting fruit, choose fresh, ripe specimens as these have more flavour and are much easier for young children to digest. And you don't have to buy seedless grapes; you can always deseed your own, but it does take time (don't forget to skin them).

ORANGEY APPLES AND BANANA

Age	3 months upwards
Preparation time	5 minutes
Cooking time	10 minutes
Serves	2

INGREDIENTS

¼ apple
¼ banana
½ teaspoon orange juice
¼ teaspoon honey

METHOD

1. Core the apple and then peel and chop it finely. Steam the apple for 10 minutes until tender then purée or mash it together with the banana, orange juice and honey.
2. Serve as soon as possible.

TIP

Alternatively, you can poach the apple in a little water or milk which will aid the mashing process.

CRÊPES – THE BASIC MIX

Age   1 year upwards
Preparation time   15 minutes
Cooking time   5 minutes
Makes about 10 crêpes

Crêpes, or pancakes, make particularly good
breakfast foods – perhaps do them when you've got a little more time
than normal to prepare them and to wash up. On the next two pages I have provided a
recipe for both a savoury and a sweet crêpe; these are ideas on which
you can base your own dishes. A good basic pancake batter is as follows:

INGREDIENTS

4 oz (100g) wholemeal flour
1 large egg
½ pint (300ml) milk
3 teaspoons of sunflower or other
   vegetable oil

METHOD

1. Sieve the flour and beat it into the egg, little by little. Add the milk slowly to keep the mixture soft.
2. When all the milk is added beat in 2 teaspoonfuls of oil and ensure that the mixture is free of lumps.
3. Heat another teaspoonful of oil in a non-stick pan and when it starts to smoke pour it off into a heat-resistant container.
4. Put a small ladle of batter (or enough to make a very thin circle) into the pan to cover the bottom.
5. Put straight onto a high heat and cook until the mix in the pan changes to a darker colour (usually 1–1½ minutes).
6. When the mixture is ready and the edges are curling a little, turn the pancake and cook the other side.
7. Serve the pancake on a clean plate ... repeat the process.

CRÊPES WITH FRUIT FILLINGS

Age	1 year onwards
Preparation time	15 minutes
Cooking time	5 minutes
Makes enough for about 10 crêpes	

Fruit-filled crêpes are ideal for breakfast.
For this recipe use the basic batter mix as on page 29. Choose whatever
fruit you wish. My personal favourites are bananas, apples, pears and seedless grapes. Just
choose anything that gets you away from the idea that crêpes (pancakes)
are a once-a-year speciality and can only be eaten with lemon juice and sugar – nice
though that combination is.

INGREDIENTS

*ingredients as for basic batter (see
   page 29)*
fruits of your choice
5 oz (125g) sugar
¹/₂ pint (300ml) water

METHOD

1. Follow the basic recipe to make pancakes.
2. Wash, peel and chop the fruit(s). Purée the banana and poach the firmer fruits, such as the apples, pears and plums, in sugar syrup for 10–15 minutes.
3. Bring the sugar and water to the boil, add the fruits and simmer for 10–15 minutes till tender.
4. Purée the fruit in your food processor/liquidizer.
5. Place a tablespoonful of the purée along one edge of the pancake, roll up and serve.

TIP

Crêpes can be good at any time. You can make them up in large batches and then freeze them. To do this, place a piece of greaseproof paper between each one to prevent them sticking together when freezing.

SCOTTISH PANCAKES

Age	1 year upwards
Preparation time	10 minutes
Cooking time	4 minutes
Makes 12–16 pancakes	

INGREDIENTS

8 oz (225g) plain wholemeal flour
1 teaspoon cream of tartar
¼ teaspoon bicarbonate of soda
pinch of salt
1 egg
1 tablespoon corn oil
8 fl oz (225ml) water
4 tablespoons skimmed milk
  powder

METHOD

1. Sift together the flour, cream of tartar, soda and salt and make a well in the centre.
2. Add the egg, oil, half of the water, and the milk powder. Mix to a smooth batter and gradually beat in the remaining water. The batter should be thick and smooth.
3. Heat a heavy-based frying pan and grease lightly. Drop in tablespoons of the batter and cook for about 2 minutes until the surface begins to bubble.
4. Turn, using a palette knife, and cook for 1–2 minutes until the underside is golden brown.
5. Keep repeating the process, placing the pancakes inside a clean folded tea-towel to keep moist until they are all cooked.

TIP

The pancakes should be served warm and are great for breakfast topped with jam or some ripe banana. For a more savoury snack, serve with a slice of cheese or cottage cheese and chives.

CRÊPES WITH SCRAMBLED EGGS AND SMOKED SALMON

Age	2 upwards
Preparation time	15 minutes
Cooking time	15 minutes
Serves	1

What – smoked salmon for a baby?
It sounds extravagant but I had to put this one in because we buy whole
sides of smoked salmon and therefore have lots of little trimmings left over which I use for
various things – this recipe included.

INGREDIENTS

some basic pancake batter
1 large egg
1 oz (25g) smoked salmon
   trimmings
fresh chives
semi-skimmed milk
vegetable oil

METHOD

1. Follow the basic recipe to make pancakes (see page 29).
2. Chop a few chives very finely and mix them into the egg, milk and smoked salmon.
3. Put the mixture into a pan containing about a teaspoonful of hot oil.
4. Briskly whisk with a fork until the mixture thickens up and starts to scramble.
5. Keep the pan moving all the time and continue to mix with the fork.
6. When the eggs are lightly scrambled, fill a pancake with the mixture and roll tightly.
7. Cut into small pieces and serve.

TIP

Some fish stalls (on markets) sell smoked salmon trimmings at a very reasonable price. Also, save a piece for yourself!

LIVER CASSEROLE

Age	6 months upwards
Preparation time	10 minutes
Cooking time	10–15 minutes
Serves	1

INGREDIENTS

a few drops of oil
¼ small onion
1 small piece lamb, calf or chicken
  liver
½ tomato (skinned)
water

METHOD

1. Peel and chop the onion and cook in a few drops of heated oil in a non-stick frying pan. Allow to soften, stirring to prevent sticking.
2. Wash, dry and cube the liver into 1-inch pieces and add it to the onion which should now be soft. Gently fry on all sides and then add the tomato and continue to cook gently.
3. Cook for 5 minutes and then cut one piece of liver open. It should be pale pink in colour, but not quite brown, all the way through. You may add a little water to prevent the liver from sticking to the surface of the pan.
4. When the liver is cooked, add enough water to dissolve any juices sticking to the bottom of the pan, and simmer gently for another 3–4 minutes.
5. Remove from the heat, peel off the tomato skin and roughly purée the mixture adding extra water if it seems too thick.

TIP

Make sure the liver is not too pink, although you do not want to overcook it or it will lose its moisture and vital nutrients.

HONEY MUESLI MUNCH

Age	2 years upwards
Preparation time	15 minutes
Cooking time	30–35 minutes
Serves	6

These make very tasty snacks,
treats or party-type food but can also be used as an addition (broken
in smaller pieces) to a more savoury breakfast cereal.

INGREDIENTS

3 tablespoons sunflower oil
3 tablespoons clear honey
12 oz (350g) unsweetened muesli
1 oz (25g) dried banana chips

METHOD

1. Gently heat the oil and honey in a saucepan until blended. Stir in the muesli and mix until well coated.
2. Turn the mixture into a large tin and bake in a hot, preheated oven (C) for 35 minutes, taking it out to stir occasionally for all-over browning.
3. Leave to cool and start to break into small pieces.
4. If you prefer to work with a finer mixture, blend in a food processor to the desired consistency before baking. Roughly break up the banana chips and stir in to the mixture.
5. Break into small pieces when cool and serve as snacks.

TIP

An excellent variation is to use strawberries in a strawberry munch! For this, place 2 tablespoons of yoghurt in each individual bowl. Add 2 oz (50g) sliced strawberries to each, then sprinkle with the Muesli Munch.

FACE BREAKFAST

Age	18 months upwards
Preparation time	15 minutes
Cooking time	5 minutes
Serves	1

When I'm cooking for larger people
presentation is of vital importance. People 'eat with their eyes' and therefore
every effort is made to make everything at The Pink Geranium look special. When you
cook for your children the appearance of the food is of equal importance.
If it looks like a 'mush' your child may treat it accordingly. If you take a little time and
thought you will be amazed what a difference it makes. What we are
making here is a basic mixed grill – prepared to look like a face.

INGREDIENTS

1 tomato
½ slice of wholemeal toast
1 egg
1 rasher of lean bacon
unsalted butter

METHOD

1. Cut the tomato in half (peel if skin appears thick), derind the bacon and cut half a slice of bread for toasting.
2. Grill (and toast) the above ingredients and keep warm while frying the egg in a little unsalted butter.
3. Serve the ingredients on a warm plate with the tomato halves as eyes, the egg as the nose, bacon the mouth and toast as hair.

TIP

The reason I have recommended 18 months onwards for this one is because it is then that children become aware of things like a face and they appreciate the various colours and textures of the food. With the same ingredients it's not hard to make a plausible looking truck ... think about it.

STEVEN'S YOGHURT

Age	3 months upwards
Preparation time	10 minutes
Cooking time	10 minutes
Serves	3

INGREDIENTS

1¼ pints (1.25l) long-life skimmed
   milk
1 heaped tablespoon dried
   skimmed milk
1 teaspoon plain low-fat yoghurt

METHOD

1. Pour the milk into a saucepan and heat until it is hot, but not quite at boiling point, although if you do use fresh milk, it must reach boiling point to kill off any bacteria.
2. Meanwhile, sterilize a mixing bowl with boiling water to ensure that the only bacteria you culture are the ones from the yoghurt, and that the containers are warm enough to activate the milk culture when it is added.
3. Stir the dried milk into the hot liquid milk. The dried milk enriches the flavour and gives the bacteria extra nutrients to feed on. Leave to cool until the temperature reaches 47°C. (If you do not have a cooking thermometer, test with your little finger: it should be able to stay in the hot milk for five seconds.)
4. Place the yoghurt into the mixing bowl and mix in a little of the milk, then add the remaining milk and stir. Cover the mixing bowl with cling film, wrap in a thick towel and place in a warm, draught-free place such as an airing cupboard overnight.
5. Once the yoghurt is set, refrigerate. This yoghurt can be used as the culture for successive batches over several weeks.

TIP

If you're a keen cook, making yoghurt is no ordeal and seems to be a better product when homemade, although this does not mean you should avoid bought yoghurts, which can also be very good.

PORRIDGE OATS WITH BANANA AND MANGO

Age	1–4 years
Preparation time	10 minutes
Cooking time	10 minutes
Serves	1

I am always suggesting that you make everything up freshly, choosing not to use packets or tins. In the case of porridge oats, however, you are well advised to buy a good brand and cook them as instructed. This is another breakfast recipe that includes the nutritious and tasty banana. Most children love them.

INGREDIENTS

1 small banana (sliced)
½ fresh mango (or alternative fruit)
2 oz (50g) porridge oats
cow's milk

METHOD

1. Make up the porridge according to the instructions on the packet.
2. Wash, peel and chop the mango and purée with the sliced banana, either with a fork or in a liquidizer.
3. Serve the porridge warm with a generous 'dollop' of the purée in the centre.

TIP

You may cook your porridge with either sugar or salt. With this recipe, try to limit the amount of both that you use. The banana and mango both have a good taste which will disguise any blandness in the oats.

MUFFINS WITH MUSHROOMS, BEEF TOMATOES AND CHEDDAR CHEESE FLAVOURED WITH TARRAGON

Age	1–4 years
Preparation time	5 minutes
Cooking time	5 minutes
Serves	2

Muffins are delicious – buy them, don't worry about making them. I tried it once and they were hard work to say the least. This recipe is one that contains a couple of ingredients that children don't always like – mushrooms and tomatoes for example. My policy is to assume that kids like everything; I certainly never suggest that there may be items they will dislike. If, having had a go, they really find a taste disagreeable, I give them something else, but children's tastes vary so much.

INGREDIENTS

1 oz (25g) brown cap organic mushrooms (or similar)
1 ripe beef tomato
1 oz (25g) Cheddar cheese
fresh tarragon
2 muffins

METHOD

1. Place a few sliced mushrooms on each muffin.
2. Place the sliced beef tomato on top of this.
3. Sprinkle with fresh tarragon and then with grated cheese.
4. Grill under a medium grill for 3 minutes and serve when warm.

TIP

Use ordinary tomatoes instead of the large beef tomatoes if you wish, and try field mushrooms (or any other sort) if you can't get the brown cap variety. I have simply recommended what I would choose to use.

BASKETS OF SCRAMBLED EGG

Age	18 months upwards
Preparation time	5 minutes
Cooking time	8–10 minutes
Serves	3

INGREDIENTS

3 slices wholemeal bread
1 oz (25g) unsalted butter
1 teaspoon oil
1 large tomato
2 eggs
salt and pepper to taste

METHOD

1. Remove the crusts from the bread and roll the slices lightly with a rolling pin, so that they bend more easily.
2. Spread one side of the bread with butter, then lightly grease 3 patty tins with butter.
3. Press the bread, buttered side up, into the tins to form a basket shape. Bake in a high preheated oven (C) for 8–10 minutes, until crisp.
4. Heat the oil in a frying pan.
5. Beat the eggs together add the chopped tomato and season with a little salt and pepper. Add to the pan and cook, stirring constantly, until scrambled.
6. Place the bread baskets on 3 individual plates and divide the filling between them.

TIP

You can, of course, use many different fillings for this recipe. One of my favourites is scrambled egg and smoked salmon, although this is more expensive to make.

PORRIDGE COOKIES

Age	1–4 years
Preparation time	10 minutes
Cooking time	30 minutes
Makes about 20 cookies	

If you have a difficult child –
and let's face it they all have their days – and she bluntly refuses cereals,
toast or any of the other goodies in this chapter – try this one. These cookies are also great
when she screams for a biscuit but you want to give her something healthy.

INGREDIENTS

4 oz (100g) porridge oats
4 oz (100g) rolled oats
1 oz (25g) smooth peanut oil
4 fl oz (100ml) sunflower oil
2 tablespoons of clear honey
3 tablespoons malt extract

METHOD

1. Put the honey, oil and malt in a pan and heat gently.
2. Remove from the heat and add remaining ingredients, mix thoroughly.
3. Press into a greased baking tin and smooth over the top with a palette knife.
4. Bake in a medium preheated oven (B) for 30 minutes until golden brown.
5. Cool for a few minutes and then cut into pieces.

TIP

You can cut the cookies into any shape or size such as simple shapes of stars, the moon, etc.
For older children use a little more imagination and create various shapes such as animals,
letters and numbers, etc.

DRIED FRUIT SPREAD

Age	6 months upwards
Preparation time	variable
Cooking time	20 minutes
Serves	2

Dried fruits have become very popular recently.
This spread makes use of them in a new sort of way – it can be used
to replace jams and marmalades at breakfast time with the knowledge that it is a purer,
more nutritious option.

INGREDIENTS

3½ dried peaches or other dried fruit
water to cover

METHOD

1. Place the peaches in a mixing bowl, cover with water and soak according to the instructions on the packet. Turn into a saucepan, bring to the boil, reduce the heat and simmer until the peaches are soft – about 20 minutes.
2. Purée or rub through a sieve, and refrigerate. This will last for a few days in the fridge – if not eaten up before!

TIP

Although fresh fruit can be used for this, dried fruits produce a thicker, sweeter, more spreadable result. Other dried fruit such as apricots, apples, pears and prunes can be used instead of peaches. This spread is excellent for making your own fruit yoghurts (see yoghurt page 36).

FROMAGE FRAIS FRUIT SPREAD

Age	3 months upwards
Preparation time	2 minutes
Cooking time	none
Serves	2

INGREDIENTS

2 oz (50g) fruit spread
2 oz (50g) fromage frais or curd
   cheese

METHOD

Mix the ingredients together well and chill. Spread the curd straight onto toast or bread.

TIP

As a baby gets a taste for this, gradually increase the proportion of cheese/fromage frais to fruit: 3 oz (75g) of cheese and 1 oz (25g) of fruit spread.

3
JUST A QUICK SNACK

INTRODUCTION

I believe that children need help in formulating taste and healthy eating habits, but they don't need a strict set of rules – at least not from me. The best way to guide them is by example, and by providing them with the opportunity to make up their own minds about what is healthy and what they like – hopefully the same thing.

Recently I spent an afternoon at the house of a friend who has two children aged three years and eighteen months. I was horrified by the amount of junk food snacks they had consumed by the time I left two hours later. They ate crisps, chocolate, lollies, crisps again, etc., enough to make them sick and me feel ill.

I would not think of interfering with the situation in somebody else's home, but I did make a policy of giving these same children some of my own snacks when they returned the visit some months later, and they appeared to enjoy them just as much.

Remember, it is snacking on junk foods that is a major cause of tooth decay in young children. So if you are providing snacks (and they are so handy if you want to give children a little treat or keep them occupied for a few moments), then try to choose those which are least likely to cause decay, such as the ones suggested here, and ignore many of the sugary ones that you can buy from the supermarket.

FINGER FOODS (SOME IDEAS)

Age	6 months upwards
Preparation time	5 minutes
Cooking time	none
Serves	various (your choice)

From the age of 6–7 months your baby will be very keen
to pick up objects, so why not encourage this with 'finger foods' which
not only teach a baby to handle and control her fingers, but are also
a very useful way of pacifying a very hungry baby who is waiting for her food!

Here are some suitable finger foods:

1. Banana chunks
2. Apple peeled, cored and quartered
3. Melon chunks (and most fruits in chunks)
4. Bread sticks and just bread
5. Florets of broccoli (cooked)
6. Strips of cooked courgette (and other vegetables, like cauliflower)
7. Grated raw carrot and cooked carrot strips
8. Cooked pasta shapes
9. Small slices of cheese or cheese triangles
10. Rusks and soft toast fingers
11. Fresh strawberries (the wonder fruit!) they are the most nutritious fruit – give them as many as they can eat!

TIP

Of course there are many other types of finger foods like slices of pizza, sandwich soldiers, and many varieties of fruits and vegetables, but to me finger foods are about what you have available at the time when a baby is crying and needs feeding. She won't always wait patiently for her lunch or dinner so it is a good idea to have a few of these ideas up your sleeve.

FINGER PITTA BREADS

Age	6 months upwards
Preparation time	10 minutes
Cooking time	none
Serves	various (your choice)

Finger-sized pitta breads
are not always easy to find in the shops, but once you have identified
a source, be sure to always keep some in the cupboard. These small pittas are ideal for
snacks; I've used them time and time again with all sorts of fillings from
taramasalata to cottage cheese. And if you can't get hold of finger pittas you can probably
find mini pittas almost anywhere.

The following are just a few ideas. The knack is to make the fillings colourful as well
as tasty, perhaps getting the children to help you in their preparation.

1. Finger pittas with Jarlsberg cheese and sultanas (grated Jarlsberg is delicious – but of
   course many other cheeses can be used)
2. Finger pittas with fromage frais
3. Finger pittas with homemade lemon curd and strawberries
4. Finger pittas with paté
5. Finger pittas with Marmite
6. Finger pittas with honey or jam

TIP

You know your child better than anybody, so you will know how confident she is about
feeding herself, and how confident you are about letting her. When my two were young,
Sally and I always watched them in case they started choking. Happily we had no scares.
Should your child choke, immediately put her over your knee (face down) and give her
several hard slaps between the shoulder blades to dislodge the object. Remove any
remaining morsels from her mouth with your fingers.

TURKISH HUMMUS

Age	18 months upwards
Preparation time	15 minutes
Cooking time	none
Serves	4

INGREDIENTS

14 oz (375g) can chick peas
1 clove of garlic
2 tablespoons lemon juice
1 tablespoon olive or corn oil
a little water
paprika pepper
parsley or mint

METHOD

1. Drain and thoroughly rinse the chick peas, and then place them with the crushed garlic, lemon juice and oil in a food blender. Blend until smooth, adding enough water to make a good, creamy consistency.
2. Pack into suitable plastic containers, garnished with a sprinkle of paprika powder and some chopped parsley or fresh mint.
3. Serve with pitta bread and vegetable sticks.

TIP

Avoid using the paprika pepper for younger children and perhaps slightly reduce the garlic and lemon content.

ORIENTAL STYLE CHICKEN

Age	2 years upwards
Preparation time	10 minutes
Cooking time	5 minutes
Serves	8

INGREDIENTS

12 oz (325g) boneless chicken
   breasts
4 oz (100g) self-raising flour
2 tablespoons toasted sesame seeds
6 fl oz (200ml) water
oil for deep frying
1 teaspoon soy sauce

METHOD

1. Skin the chicken and cut into cubes, season with pepper and salt.
2. Mix together the flour, sesame seeds and a little salt, then gradually stir in the water to form a smooth batter.
3. Stir in the chicken making sure each piece is well coated.
4. Heat the oil. You will know when it is hot enough by dropping a little batter into the pan, it should rise and start to brown immediately.
5. Cook the chicken a few pieces at a time, until golden brown. Drain as much of the oil from the meat once well cooked.
6. The chicken bites should be served warm, with the soy sauce mixed into a tomato sauce (see page 72) for dipping.

TIP

You could serve mayonnaise as a dipping-sauce mixed with a little tomato sauce to make it pink.

SURPRISE MEATBALLS

Age	1 year upwards
Preparation time	10 minutes
Cooking time	12 minutes
Serves	2

I love meatballs because there seem to be endless variations to try out. These ones look appealing to children, taste delicious and really don't take long to prepare. They also freeze very well and make wonderful afternoon cold snacks when pre-cooked.

INGREDIENTS

½ lb (225g) chicken breast
1 oz (25g) Cheddar cheese (cubed)
1 egg
1 oz (25g) unsalted butter
a few chopped chives
2 tablespoons wholemeal flour

METHOD

1. Mince the chicken meat and add the egg and butter (you can season with a little salt). Sprinkle a few chopped chives in with the mixture.
2. Mould into ball shapes (the size of a walnut) and press a cube of the cheese into the centre of each ball.
3. Shape back into a ball again and roll in a little flour.
4. Either deep or (preferably) shallow fry the balls in a little oil on a fairly low heat until golden brown, turning them all the time for 10–12 minutes.

TIP

If you do shallow fry the meatballs, seal them so they are nice and brown and then finish them off in a hot oven (B) for 10 minutes. Serve warm.

CHICKEN PARFAÏT

Age	6 months upwards
Preparation time	10 minutes
Cooking time	25 minutes
Serves	3

A parfaït is similar to a paté but smoother.
In this recipe we purée the livers to form a smooth rich paté.

INGREDIENTS

8 oz (225g) chicken livers
3 good-sized sprigs of parsley
3½ tablespoons orange or tomato
    juice
1 medium onion
a little stock or water with a
    dessertspoon of lemon juice
    added
1 clove garlic

METHOD

1. Place the livers and parsley in a mixing bowl, and pour over the orange or tomato juice.
2. Place the peeled and chopped onion and garlic in a small saucepan, and add the stock or water and lemon juice. Bring to the boil, reduce the heat and simmer until the onion is tender, stirring to prevent sticking.
3. Add the liver mixture, bring to simmering point again and cook for about 10 minutes, or until the outsides of the livers are browned and the insides still slightly pink.
4. Drain off the cooking liquid and reserve. Blend the liver in a food processor, with about half the reserved cooking liquid, until smooth. Chill well before using.

TIP

Try not to overcook the liver or it becomes dry and bitter-tasting. You can also make the same paté using duck livers if you prefer a stronger flavour. Ask your butcher to remove all the sinews, skin and gall bladder for you.

SALMON MUFFINS

Age	1 year upwards
Preparation time	5 minutes
Cooking time	10 minutes
Serves	2

Although it sounds exotic,
salmon is not as expensive as one might expect, and you can always
use off-cuts from your own dinner for this recipe. Alternatively, of course, you can use up
bits and pieces of other fish or even meat (like ham) for this tasty dish.

INGREDIENTS

4 oz (100g) cottage cheese
4 oz (100g) lightly cooked salmon
1 tomato
3 wholemeal muffins
2 oz (50g) mild Cheddar cheese

METHOD

1. Skin and chop the tomato. Then mix it with the cottage cheese and salmon.
2. Spread the mixture over the muffins and sprinkle this with grated cheese.
3. Bake (or grill) in a low preheated (A) oven for 10 minutes, or until they are golden brown.

TIP

You can use fromage frais as an alternative to cottage cheese, and by adding assorted chopped vegetables (such as mushrooms) you can reduce the amount of salmon required to perhaps just 1 oz (25g)! And you can also use bread rolls instead of muffins if preferred.

DANISH FRITTERS

Age	1 year upwards
Preparation time	15 minutes
Cooking time	15 minutes
Serves	6

These fritters are a good way of ensuring your children eat meat. Perhaps serve them with a dip, such as the spicy cheese and tomato dip on page 123.

INGREDIENTS

8 oz (225g) stewing beef
8 oz (225g) diced chicken
3 oz (75g) onions
4 oz (100g) flour
salt
freshly ground pepper
1 egg
1/2 pint (300ml) milk
vegetable oil (enough for deep
    frying)
chopped parsley and herbs

METHOD

1. Peel and slice the onion and then mince this with the beef and chicken. Add the herbs.
2. Meanwhile, make a batter by sifting the flour and seasoning it before blending in the egg and milk.
3. Stir the meat and onion mixture into the batter and leave to stand for about 1 hour.
4. Slowly heat about 1/4 inch of oil in a frying pan.
5. Gently place teaspoonfuls of the mixture into the pan. On a low heat, fry for about 15 minutes, turning from time to time, until the batter is crisp.
6. Ensure that the meat is well cooked; once happy that it is, serve immediately.

TIP

Fritters are a good way of using up leftovers such as beef or lamb from Sunday lunch. Otherwise buy a cheap cut of meat and mince finely with the onions, parsley and chives.

SATÉ BREAD

Age	9 months upwards
Preparation time	10 minutes
Cooking time	5 minutes
Serves	2

The sweet taste of smooth peanut butter covers up the very savoury flavours of what would otherwise be 'eggy bread'. Both my girls think this is a wonderful snack. Serena actually called it saté bread from a very young age and understood that saté meant peanut, so she was getting an education with her food!

INGREDIENTS

2 slices thick white bread
a little unsalted butter
2 teaspoons smooth peanut butter
1 egg

METHOD

1. Spread the peanut butter over the bread lightly on both sides.
2. Beat the egg a little to combine the white and the yolk. Dip the bread into the egg and allow it to soak in.
3. Gently fry the bread in a little unsalted butter for a few minutes each side; cut off crusts and serve.

TIP

Please note that I use white bread in this and other recipes. The fibre in brown bread can sometimes stop the absorption of iron into the body – so be careful not to feed your child too much fibre. Also ensure you use smooth peanut butter spread, not the crunchy sort.

TARRAGON EGGS 'EN COCOTTE'

The word Cocotte refers to a round or oval individual casserole traditionally made of earthenware. In this recipe we use a ramekin dish which is the next best thing

Age	18 months upwards
Preparation time	10 minutes
Cooking time	10 minutes
Serves	4

The flavour of tarragon goes well with eggs; you could try adding just a little fresh tarragon to scrambled eggs or an omelette for example. In this recipe, the meal is not only high in taste, but it is also very nutritious.

INGREDIENTS

4 eggs
8 tablespoons fresh double cream
2 teaspoons fresh tarragon
   (chopped)
salt
freshly ground pepper

METHOD

1. Butter four ramekin dishes (see the tip) and break an egg into each.
2. Mix the fresh cream, the tarragon and a little salt and freshly ground pepper in a basin.
3. Spoon 2 tablespoons of this mixture onto each yolk and cover with foil.
4. These are then cooked on the top of the oven by standing the ramekins in nearly boiling water, up to about three-quarters submerged, in a thick-based shallow pan (a frying pan is ideal).
5. Keep the water topped up and simmer for about 10 minutes. These are ready when the egg whites are set but the yolks are still soft.

TIP

Ramekin dishes are excellent for mousselines (see page 116) and other recipes where individual portions are being cooked in the oven. Children often like to have their own portion. If you don't have ramekin dishes, you can use other pots or moulds approximately 2–3 inches in diameter.

TRADITIONAL WELSH RAREBIT

Age	18 months upwards
Preparation time	10 minutes
Cooking time	10 minutes
Serves	4

This traditional favourite is a useful teatime snack.
You can make tiny rounds of toast (using a pastry cutter) for an attractive presentation.

INGREDIENTS

4 slices of bread
2 oz (50g) unsalted butter
8 oz (225g) Cheddar cheese
¼ pint (150ml) beer (optional)
½ level teaspoon paprika
1 teaspoon mustard powder
2 egg yolks (beaten)

METHOD

1. Remove the crusts from the bread and toast lightly.
2. Melt the butter over a very low heat and then add the cheese and beer. You are aiming to produce a smooth, moderately thick sauce.
3. Add the paprika, mustard and the beaten egg yolks. Do not let the mixture boil, but bring up to a good heat before pouring over the toast; serve immediately.

TIP

You can produce similarly good results if you omit the beer and use Worcestershire sauce. And if you're using beer, don't worry; the alcohol cooks out.

FRESH HERB MELBA TOAST

Age	1 year upwards
Preparation time	5 minutes
Cooking time	5 minutes
Serves	2

Serena was only 6 months old
when she started craving for food in the afternoons, soon after lunch!
We wanted to feed her something but obviously wanted to avoid junk food and chocolate,
etc. The first 'snack' I ever gave Serena was a small piece of melba toast
from the restaurant. She loved it and it kept her quiet for a long time. This recipe is easy.

INGREDIENTS

2 slices white bread
a few chopped herbs: chives,
*   tarragon, parsley and basil (or*
*   other fresh, soft green herbs)*

METHOD

1. Toast your bread, remove crusts and slice in half, lengthways.
2. Rub each slice together lightly to remove the 'fluffy' bits and then sprinkle the soft side with a few freshly chopped herbs. (Don't use too many herbs or it will be overpowering.)
3. Put under a hot grill until golden brown and toast starts curling up. Serve cold.

TIP

Parsley contains three times the vitamin C of oranges – use it liberally in any foods. And white bread contains calcium, making it generally better for your baby's teeth than brown.

4
STOCKS, SOUPS AND SAUCES

INTRODUCTION

In my experience a lot of children seem to dislike soups, not because of their flavour but because they think they're being shortchanged on a meal. At first glance a soup seems to be insubstantial . . . and worse than that, perhaps a bit boring.

Of course I've never produced a boring soup in my life! Children need to be tempted and teased. This can be done with interesting toppings, swirls of yoghurt and tasty accompanying breads. Once tempted, the children will soon be hooked on the taste.

From a parent's point of view, soups offer many advantages. They can be good for using up odd bits and pieces and are therefore quite economical, they can be stored quite easily and they provide an effective way of ensuring that your child receives plenty of nourishment and goodness. You may also find that your children will happily eat items like leeks and carrots in soup form that they won't touch if served as a vegetable.

COOKING TECHNIQUES

With soups we are looking to keep all the nutritional value of the ingredients in the final liquid. We may be boiling off a lot of water when 'reducing' the soups and we will also discard the remains of some of the solid ingredients when making a purée. The key is to always retain the liquid part of the preparation – the cooking liquor – as herein lies the flavour and the goodness. Even if some of it is left over at the end it can be stored for a few days for possible use in some other meal.

In this chapter I talk about the techniques of 'reduction' and 'sweating'. Reduction is the reducing of the liquid content of soup by boiling in an open pan to intensify the flavour. It needs to be done under reasonably regular supervision to ensure the liquid doesn't boil over or boil dry. Sweating is a way of cooking food gently in melted fat in a covered pan; it is done for a few minutes only, until the juices begin to run.

STOCKS

I have started this chapter with three basic stocks, all mildly flavoured, which are ideal for using as a base for other soups, or which can be used as soups in their own right. I always have at least one made-up stock in my refrigerator. Stocks are very versatile, an essential part of good cooking for both adults and children.

Vegetable Stock

Age   6 months upwards
Preparation time   5 minutes
Cooking time   60 minutes
Makes 1 pint

A basic vegetable stock is a very useful item
to have in your fridge. It has many uses in cooking, for sauces, soups
and diluting. It hardly needs stating, but there is plenty of goodness in a stock like this.

INGREDIENTS

1 small onion
1 small carrot
1 small leek
a few button mushrooms
unsalted butter
3 pints (1.725l) of water
*1 bunch chervil or tarragon (not
    essential)*

METHOD

1. Roughly chop the vegetables.
2. Add these to a melted knob of butter in a thick-bottomed saucepan. Fry gently for 2 minutes.
3. Pour on three pints (1.725l) of cold water and bring to the boil. Add the herbs.
4. Once boiled, skim, reduce heat and simmer for ¾ hour.
5. Sieve through a strainer, pressing hard with the back of a spoon or ladle to extract as many of the juices from the vegetables as possible.
6. Put the stock back onto the boil and reduce again by half to concentrate the flavour.

TIP

You can use whatever fresh vegetables you have, or just use the ends or trimmings. Do not use overpowering vegetables like peppers. If you store the stock in a clean airtight glass jar it will keep in the fridge for up to a week.

LIGHT CHICKEN STOCK

Age	6 months upwards
Preparation time	15 minutes
Cooking time	60 minutes
Makes 1 pint	

Garlic for children?
If it's good for *your* health then it must be good for your children's. This
recipe has a little more flavour than the vegetable stock, but is still quite mild. Ideal for use
in the preparation of other meals, and also as a soup with a little wholemeal
bread.

INGREDIENTS

2lb (900g) chicken wings or carcass
unsalted butter
1 small leek
1 small onion
1 small stalk of celery
3 oz (75g) mushrooms or
  mushroom stalks
1 clove garlic
½ pint (300ml) of water
1 sprig parsley
½ fresh bayleaf

METHOD

1. Gently fry (sweat) the chicken wings and/or carcass in a little butter in a large saucepan, without colouring for two or three minutes.
2. Roughly chop the vegetables and garlic and add them to the chicken. Let them sweat for another 5 minutes.
3. Pour in about ½ pint (300ml) of cold water and boil to reduce by one third.
4. Skim and add herbs, simmer for 1 hour, skimming from time to time.
5. Strain through a fine sieve and leave stock to cool.

TIP

You can freeze the stock for up to 2 months (to hold nutritional value) or keep in your fridge for up to 4 days. When freezing, store in ice-cube trays and then you can take as much or as little stock as required.

LIGHT FISH STOCK

Age	6 months upwards
Preparation time	15 minutes
Cooking time	30 minutes
Makes 1 pint	

Using white fish bones ensures
that this is a very light stock, ideal as a base for fish soups, fish sauces
and for adding to any meal for extra flavour and nourishment.

INGREDIENTS

1 lb (450g) fish bones
1 onion
1 leek
1 carrot
¼ celery stalk
3 oz (75g) mushrooms or
    mushroom stalks (optional)
unsalted butter
½ pint (300ml) of water
small bunch parsley

METHOD

1. Peel and slice the onion and wash and dice the other vegetables. Place these in a large saucepan with a little butter and fry gently (sweat) for up to 2 minutes.
2. Add the fish bones and sweat for another 2 minutes.
3. Pour in about ½ pint (300ml) of water, bring to the boil and boil for 2 minutes.
4. Skim and simmer for 15–20 minutes.
5. Finally, strain through a metal sieve, pressing the bones with the back of a ladle.

TIP

I know it is very tempting to use stock cubes for convenience, but generally they are too highly seasoned for children, and, in any case, I don't know of any fish stock cubes.

AVOCADO AND PRAWN SOUP

Age	3 years upwards
Preparation time	20 minutes
Cooking time	none
Serves	8

A cold soup with a favourite combination of flavours
but you can substitute prawns for any other fish you have available.

INGREDIENTS

2 large ripe avocados
2 tablespoons lemon juice
1 pint (575ml) chicken stock, cold
½ pint (300ml) milk
salt
Worcestershire sauce
2 fl oz (50ml) mayonnaise
2 fl oz (50ml) fresh single cream
1–2 tablespoons tomato ketchup
2 oz (50g) prawns

METHOD

1. Squeeze the lemons and add the juice to the avocados. Mash the two together using a fork.
2. Add the stock and milk and whisk.
3. Season with salt, and Worcestershire sauce. If at this stage the soup is too thick, then dilute with extra milk.
4. Chill well.
5. In a separate bowl, mix together the cream and mayonnaise.
6. Peel and chop the prawns then stir them into the mixture together with the tomato sauce and a little more Worcestershire sauce if desired.
7. Season to taste and serve.

TIP

Avocado makes a useful and nutritious base for cold soup and sauces and can be enjoyed by all of the family.

CREAM OF FRESH TOMATO AND BASIL SOUP

Age	3 months upwards
Preparation time	10 minutes
Cooking time	20 minutes
Serves	2

I've often wondered why manufacturers
of tinned tomato soup don't produce one flavoured with basil. Basil
and tomatoes are married! By that I mean they complement each other beautifully and
should be seen together more often in my opinion.

INGREDIENTS

2 large tomatoes
6 tablespoons vegetable stock
1 tablespoon natural yoghurt
4 tablespoons milk
2 medium-sized basil leaves
  (chopped)

METHOD

1. In a large saucepan heat the vegetable stock and reduce to nearly half.
2. Make a purée of the tomatoes by peeling them and then pressing them through a fine sieve into a clean dish.
3. Stir the milk in with the tomatoes and add the chopped basil.
4. Add this to the stock and bring to the boil.
5. Finally remove from heat and, after a few minutes (when cooler), stir in the natural yoghurt, which will both add to the flavour and help to cool the soup down.

TIP

It is easier and more economical to process/blend the tomatoes before pressing through the sieve. This way you get more out of the purée – both in amount and flavour. Don't use too much basil as it will be too strong for most children.

'PETITS-POIS' SOUP

Age	3 months upwards
Preparation time	15 minutes
Cooking time	35 minutes
Serves	4

I always try to make this soup when fresh peas
are in season because the recipe brings out superb flavours and can be
served hot or cold.

INGREDIENTS

2 oz (50g) unsalted butter
1 small onion
*2 lb (900g) fresh petits-pois (or
  frozen petits-pois if not in
  season)*
*2 pints (1.1l) vegetable or chicken
  stock*
½ teaspoon castor sugar
2 large sprigs of fresh mint
salt
2 egg yolks
¼ pint (150ml) double cream
fresh mint to garnish

METHOD

1. Shell the peas and skin and finely chop the onion.
2. Melt the butter in a large saucepan, add the onion and cook for 5 minutes until the onion is soft.
3. To this add the peas, stock, sugar and sprigs of mint. Bring to the boil and cook for about 30 minutes.
4. The soup should then be puréed using a blender.
5. Return to the pan and add the seasoning.
6. In a separate bowl, beat together the egg yolks and fresh cream and add to the soup.
7. Heat gently, whilst stirring continuously. Do not boil otherwise it will curdle.
8. Finally, transfer to a soup tureen and garnish with fresh mint.

TIP

Use frozen peas if you cannot get hold of fresh ones, it is still a delicious soup!

CREAMY CARROT AND CELERIAC SOUP

Age	1 year upwards
Preparation time	15 minutes
Cooking time	15 minutes
Serves	3

Celeriac is one of my favourite vegetables,
it has a light, creamy flavour and, blended with carrots, makes a delicious
soup. I'm always tempted to grate a little fresh nutmeg on the top – but your baby doesn't
appreciate it as much as I do!

INGREDIENTS

1 bunch of baby carrots (or 1 large
    carrot)
½ small celeriac
¼ pint (150ml) vegetable stock
½ pint (284ml) milk
1 tablespoon natural yoghurt
salt

METHOD

1. Clean, peel and cut celeriac and carrots into small pieces (about ¼-inch cubes is ideal).
2. Put the stock and the milk in a saucepan and heat.
3. Add the vegetables and just a hint of salt. Then bring to the boil.
4. Simmer for about 15 minutes.
5. Drain (keeping the cooking liquid for something else) and liquidize the carrot and celeriac.
6. Dilute with a little of the vegetable stock and finally stir in the yoghurt to give it a delicious creamy texture and flavour.

TIP

It is a good idea to cook up all the celeriac and purée it for other recipes. It will keep in the fridge for up to 4 days. Parsnip cooked in the same way is a good alternative combination with the carrot for this soup.

CAULIFLOWER AND CHEESE SOUP

Age	18 months upwards
Preparation time	20 minutes
Cooking time	60 minutes
Serves	4

This delicious winter warmer of a recipe
is right for all the family – absolutely scrumptious! If you like, you can
use blue cheese but I find it is too strong for young children.

INGREDIENTS

1 medium cauliflower
2 oz (50g) unsalted butter
1 oz (25g) flour
1/2 pint (300ml) milk
4 oz (100g) medium strength
 cheese

METHOD

1. Separate the cauliflower stalks from the florets; keep the florets for later. Next produce a stock from the stalk by boiling for about 30 minutes in water and then blending the stock in a processor.
2. Sauté the florets in melted butter and then remove them from the pan. Stir the flour and about half the stock from the stalks into the remaining butter. As the mixture thickens pour in the milk and bring to the boil.
3. Add florets to the soup and gently stir in all but 2 tablespoons of cheese. Use the remaining stock to alter consistency to taste.
4. Use the remaining cheese on the top of the soup when serving.

TIP

Do not put the extra cheese on top for very small children as it can be difficult to digest – I think that cheese is best served in small quantities.

SPINACH, ORANGE AND NUTMEG SOUP

Age	1 year upwards
Preparation time	20 minutes
Cooking time	60 minutes
Serves	6

The first time I made this was for guests in my restaurant. I had a box
of beautiful fresh spinach that I wanted to use up so I created this dish
which, at the time, I was unsure about. Its success, proved by requests for second helpings,
convinced me I was onto a winner. I have been adapting it ever since,
arriving at this version of the original, which I believe is good for all the family.

INGREDIENTS

1½ pints (900ml) vegetable stock
1½ pints (900ml) milk
2lb (900g) fresh leaf spinach
2 onions
2 oranges
2 level tablespoons flour
2 level teaspoons salt
4 oz (100g) unsalted butter
a little nutmeg (freshly grated)

METHOD

1. Wash the spinach and chop coarsely only the best, freshest leaves. Skin and finely chop the onion.
2. Shred the rind of the oranges and blanch this, by boiling for a couple of minutes. Squeeze the juice from the remainder of the oranges.
3. Melt the butter in a large pan, add the vegetables and nearly all the rind. On a low heat, cover the pan with a tight-fitting lid (or use greaseproof paper under the lid) and allow to sweat for about 10 minutes, or until soft.
4. Remove from the heat and stir in the flour, stock and milk. Return to the heat, bring to the boil, season and simmer for 15 minutes.
5. This mixture should be puréed in your processor, then reheated for serving. Just before serving, add the orange juice and garnish with the remaining rind.

TIP

To make an even creamier soup, but more extravagant you could add cream to replace the milk in stage 4 of the method.

WILD MUSHROOM SOUP WITH TARRAGON

Age	2 years upwards
Preparation time	5 minutes
Cooking time	20 minutes
Serves	2/4

Okay, so it sounds a bit exotic for a baby!
But today you can get so many different varieties of mushrooms – maybe
not wild as such, but certainly 'field' or 'organic' – that it's worth a try. Look out for
shitake or 'oyster' mushrooms if you can't see ones labelled as wild.

INGREDIENTS

4 oz (50g) mushrooms
1 sprig tarragon
1 pint (600ml) vegetable stock
2 tablespoons natural yoghurt
a few chopped chives (optional)

METHOD

1. Heat the stock and reduce slightly.
2. Add the mushrooms and tarragon and cook for 7–10 minutes.
3. Drain (keeping cooking liquid) and liquidize.
4. Dilute slightly with the cooking liquor, and blend in yoghurt with a spoon.
5. Sprinkle in a few finely chopped chives or parsley before serving.

TIP

Wild mushrooms are generally expensive but have a good full flavour. Tarragon and mushrooms are another perfect 'marriage'. Chives and/or parsley add extra vitamin C to the dish, so if you have them available, use them. Other herbs also add flavour, colour and vitamins.

SMOKED HADDOCK CHOWDER

Age	1 year
Preparation time	15 minutes
Cooking time	30 minutes
Serves	4/6

A chowder is a combination of fish and potatoes,
usually in the form of a soup. In this recipe I use smoked haddock but
you can try almost any fish providing it is undyed
and, preferably for children, unsmoked.

INGREDIENTS

1 pint (600ml) of water or milk
½lb (225g) smoked haddock fillet
4 oz (110g) potatoes
1 medium onion
1 level tablespoon flour
3 oz (80g) carrots
¼ pint (150ml) fresh single cream
or 1 carton of natural yoghurt
1 oz (25g) unsalted butter
fresh parsley
salt

METHOD

1. Simmer the fish in the water or milk until tender. This will take about 5–7 minutes. Drain off the liquid and keep it for later in the recipe.
2. Flake the fish coarsely, ensuring that any bones and skin are removed.
3. Chop the onion finely and sauté in the butter until soft. Stir in the flour and gradually add the strained fish stock. Keep stirring while bringing it to the boil.
4. Peel and dice (about ¼ inch cubes) the potatoes and coarsely grate the carrots. Add these to the stock and simmer until they are tender.
5. Stir in the fresh cream and fish, add a little seasoning and serve hot, garnished with a little chopped parsley.

TIP

For young children it is advisable to purée the potatoes and carrots so there are no lumps present; older children prefer the texture of vegetables much more.

COUNTRY VEGETABLE SOUP

Age	1 year upwards
Preparation time	15 minutes
Cooking time	35–40 minutes
Serves	4

This is a simple but tasty soup
that can double up as a base for a sauce to accompany fish or meat. If
chilled in an airtight container it will keep well – for days normally or even longer if you
omit the cream until just before serving. I usually add a selection of green
vegetables a few minutes before serving to add colour, flavour and texture.

INGREDIENTS

8 oz (225g) of assorted green
    vegetables
2 oz (50g) unsalted butter
4 oz (110g) carrots
3 oz (80g) swede
1 small leek
1 oz (25g) flour
3/4 pint (450ml) chicken stock
1/4 pint (150ml) milk
6 tablespoons fresh single cream
fresh parsley
salt
freshly ground pepper

METHOD

1. Wash and finely chop all of the vegetables.
2. Melt the butter in a large saucepan and fry the carrots,
   swede and leeks for 5–10 minutes.
3. Stir in the flour. Add the stock, salt and pepper and
   simmer for another 15–20 minutes, before adding the
   milk and fresh cream. Adjust seasoning and heat
   gently. Do not boil. Cook for a further 10–15
   minutes.
4. Pour into warmed bowls and sprinkle with parsley.
   Serve with warmed crusty bread.

TIP

If you want this to be a truly vegetarian dish, replace the chicken stock with a vegetable
stock.

GREEN LENTIL SOUP

Age	3 months upwards
Preparation time	15 minutes
Cooking time	1 hour 20 minutes
Serves	3

Lentils are actually delicious when made into a soup. Look out for *Puy* lentils (the smaller French ones) and add a few of these (cooked!) to the finished soup as a garnish.

INGREDIENTS

3½ oz (87g) green (or red) lentils
2 tablespoons oil
1 small onion
2 carrots
1 pint (575ml) chicken or vegetable stock
salt and freshly ground black pepper (optional)
milk, for thinning

METHOD

1. Thoroughly rinse the lentils and place in a saucepan with enough water to completely cover them. Boil for 15 minutes and then drain.
2. Meanwhile, heat the oil in the pan, add the peeled and chopped onion and diced carrots and cover. Allow the vegetables to sweat for about 5 minutes until the onion becomes soft.
3. Return the lentils to the pan and add the stock and seasoning. Cover and slowly bring to the boil, reduce the heat and simmer gently for up to 1 hour, or until the lentils are soft.
4. Allow to cool and then blend well with the other ingredients. Thin with milk or cream to achieve the desired consistency. Serve warm.

TIP

If you have the time, leave the lentils soaking overnight which will make them more tender than the suggested 15 minutes of boiling.

LEEK AND POTATO SOUP

Age	3 months upwards
Preparation time	10 minutes
Cooking time	40 minutes
Serves	4

INGREDIENTS

1 tablespoon oil
4 large leeks
1 large potato
1½ pints (900ml) chicken or
*   vegetable stock*
salt and freshly ground black
*   pepper*
3–4 tablespoons milk or cream

METHOD

1. Place the oil in a large saucepan and heat until it runs easily. Wash, trim and cut the leeks into fine rings and peel and chop the potato. Mix them together, add them to the pan and cover, allowing the vegetables to soften for 5 minutes.
2. Add the stock and bring to the boil. Then reduce the heat and simmer for about 30 minutes, by which time the leeks and potato should be soft and thoroughly cooked.
3. Purée the vegetables and cooking liquid in a blender and season lightly. Finally add the milk or cream; this gives the soup an extra creamy flavour and smooth consistency.

TIP

Make sure you wash the leeks thoroughly before cooking to ensure the removal of any possible soil and grit.

SIMPLE TOMATO SOUP/SAUCE

Age	3 months upwards
Preparation time	10 minutes
Cooking time	10 minutes
Serves	2

Tomato sauce is a must
if you are going to cook anything more than just the basics for your child
– and even then I couldn't do without it. It comes in so handy for giving moisture and
flavour; it is also easy to store in an airtight container and freezes well.

INGREDIENTS

1 tablespoon olive oil
1 clove garlic
1 medium onion
1½lb (675g) of fresh tomatoes (or
    tinned plum tomatoes)
salt

METHOD

1. Crush the garlic and finely chop the onion. Gently fry these in the heated oil.
2. Chop the tomatoes and season lightly with a little salt.
3. Add the tomatoes to the heated garlic and onions and cook until the mixture thickens.
4. Finally, blend or strain the sauce to extract all the juices and flavour.

TIP

Tinned tomatoes do very well for this recipe, although I prefer to use fresh ones. Do not add any herbs to this sauce if you are planning to keep it and use it for other things. Use this as a base for various soups and sauces. You can add a host of vegetables, for example, to produce a delicious soup.

BEURRE BLANC SCENTED WITH CELERY

Age	3 months upwards
Preparation time	10 minutes
Cooking time	25 minutes
Makes ¼ pint (150ml)	

This sauce can be used for a host
of vegetarian recipes but it is also particularly delicious with fish dishes.
You can substitute celery with fennel or fennel herb if you wish.

INGREDIENTS

3 sticks celery
½ pint (300ml) milk
4 oz (100g) unsalted butter (diced and chilled.)
1 tablespoon white wine vinegar
salt and pepper
a little freshly chopped fennel (or dill)

METHOD

1. The celery should be cleaned, de-stringed and very finely chopped. Place it in a saucepan with the milk and cover. Simmer gently for 15 minutes until the celery is tender.
2. Strain the mixture, reserving the milk and celery.
3. Reduce the white wine vinegar by half in a saucepan (until it is syrupy) and add 2 oz (50g) of the diced butter. Cook for 2 minutes stirring all the time.
4. Remove the pan from the heat and gradually add a little (1 fl oz) of the reserved milk.
5. Return to the heat and simmer, continuing to cook until the sauce thickens.
6. Simmer for 5 minutes and then add the reserved celery.
7. Season with salt and freshly ground white pepper and add fresh chopped herbs.
8. The remainder of the butter should be added in small knobs and beaten in well. Do not boil again.

TIP

You can replace the milk with cream for a richer sauce, but this works out more expensive.

5
Fish Dishes

Introduction

Fish, we have been told over the years, is good for the brain and therefore very good for growing children. Like many old wives' tales there is more than just a hint of truth in this. The fact is that fish is a good source of vitamin B which nourishes the nervous system, and so it's quite a valid claim to say that it's good for the brain.

Additionally, oily fish is one of the few foods that is naturally rich in vitamin D – good for the circulation and heart. Combine this with the fact that white fish in particular has a very low fat content, and that all fish are mineral rich, and you can see why the subject of this chapter comes top of many nutritionists' lists of 'super foods'.

Nutrition aside, fish also offers meals of flavour and interest. There are so many types of fish from which you can choose, and so many ways in which you can combine fish with other foods . . . and this applies to adults as well as children.

For children, you do have the problem of fish bones. It is important to ensure that the bones are removed from any dish you serve to your young child, but it is an easy job to do, particularly with cooked fish. I also have some reservations about smoked fish which can be too salty for children, although a little can add a lot of flavour to a dish – remember to use it sparingly.

My advice is, as always, to try things out. You can always eat what your child doesn't, and starting from the standpoint that children naturally love all foods, then you won't go far wrong.

A final point about fish concerns their inclusion in an otherwise vegetarian diet. I don't believe that, in the main, vegetarians want to eat fish, but I do know some vegetarian parents who allow their children small amounts of fish in their diet. They find it much less offensive than red or white meats and know that it provides plenty of nourishment.

GOUJONS OF SOLE WITH A FENNEL SAUCE

Age	1 year upwards
Preparation time	10 minutes
Cooking time	10 minutes
Serves	2

Goujons are small pieces, normally strips.
This is what I call a gentle dish, with delicate colours and flavours. The cooking is also mild, with care being taken not to overheat at any stage. Perhaps you should cook this dish when you come home from your yoga class.

INGREDIENTS

3 oz (75g) of lemon sole
2 fl oz (50ml) milk
1 sprig of fresh fennel
1 small onion/shallot
½ clove garlic (crushed)
1 dessertspoon natural yoghurt
unsalted butter
salt

METHOD

1. Cut the sole in strips (about 3 × ½ inch).
2. Melt a knob of butter in a saucepan and add the strips of fish, the crushed garlic and finely chopped onion.
3. Cook for 2–3 minutes without allowing to colour and add the milk. Simmer for about 5 minutes.
4. Remove the fish and set aside to cool.
5. Add the chopped fennel to the milk (sauce) and heat thoroughly.
6. Add the yoghurt cold and stir in before serving (it can look very nice and will help cool the dish down).
7. Finally pour the sauce over the fish and serve.

TIP

You can add puréed potato or another vegetable to the sauce to help thicken it up and to add more nourishment to the dish. Pieces of soft white bread will do the same and, at the same time, add calcium.

FILLETS OF SOLE WITH GRAPES VERONIQUE

Age	1 year upwards
Preparation time	15 minutes
Cooking time	see variable cooking methods
Serves	2

INGREDIENTS

2 fillets of sole
1 small shallot
1 oz (25g) mushrooms
1 teaspoon parsley
¼ pint (150ml) milk
1 oz (25g) unsalted butter
6 grapes

METHOD

1. Peel and finely chop the shallot and mushrooms and put together with the fillet of sole in a dish. Add the chopped parsley and pour over the milk.
2. Cook in a medium oven (B) preheated for 8–10 minutes or cover with a lid and microwave on high for 3½ minutes. Once the fish is cooked, drain off and reserve the milk.
3. Use the butter, and flavoured milk to make a sauce in the usual way. Try not to make it too thick.
4. Skin, halve and deseed the grapes and add to the sauce. Cook for a few minutes.
5. Chop the fish into pieces and pour the sauce over the fish.

TIP

If you make this for the family, you can add white wine to the sauce at stage 3 of the method. Reduce a little for good flavour.

FLAKES OF SALMON WITH CHIVE SAUCE

Age	6 months upwards
Preparation time	10 minutes
Cooking time	20 minutes
Serves	2

This is a good family dish. Everyone seems to enjoy it. I call it 'safe'!
You can cook the salmon in the same way and serve it with a multiplicity of sauces. Try, for example, salmon with celery Beurre Blanc on page 73.

INGREDIENTS

4 oz (100g) fillet of salmon
1 dessertspoon lemon juice
¹/₂ small onion
1 small tomato
a sprig of parsley
1 oz (25g) butter

CHIVE SAUCE
1 oz (25g) unsalted butter
1 dessertspoon plain flour
¹/₄ pint (150ml) milk
cooking liquid from the fish
1 dessertspoon chives

METHOD

1. Peel and slice the onion. Cut up the tomato into very small pieces and chop the parsley.
2. Add the lemon juice, bayleaf and butter. Mix all of these ingredients together and smooth over the salmon fillet.
3. Wrap the salmon in aluminium foil and bake in a medium preheated oven (B) for 15 minutes.
4. Meanwhile, make a white sauce, using the butter, flour and milk in the usual way.
5. Once the salmon is cooked, remove it from the foil, strain off the cooking liquid and add this to the white sauce.
6. Finely chop the chives and stir into the sauce.
7. Flake the cooked salmon and pour the chive sauce over it.

TIP

The tomato, onion and parsley mix can be used as a stuffing (perhaps for older children or adults) inside a fillet of salmon. Also, serve the sauce around the fish instead of all over it.

'SALMON MOUSSE' WITH SAUCE PROVENÇALE

Age   1 year upwards
Preparation time   15 minutes
Cooking time   20 minutes
Serves   6

This dish is a bit like a fish paté and can be served both hot and cold. My children love it cold with fingers of warm toast. I must admit I've used this dish as a starter many times at The Pink Geranium – each time with successful results.

INGREDIENTS

10 oz (275g) of puréed potato
3/4 oz (20g) of cooked salmon
2 tablespoons of vegetable purée
1/2 clove garlic (crushed)
2 fl oz (50ml) cream or natural
    yoghurt
salt

SAUCE

3 large tomatoes
1/2 clove garlic
1 small onion or shallot
soy sauce
2 leaves of fresh basil
water

METHOD

1. Fold the puréed potato and fish together and add the vegetable purée, garlic (crushed) and cream or yoghurt. Mix well or blend in a liquidizer.
2. Season with a little salt and put mixture into small pots in the fridge – it will keep for up to three days in a cold fridge.
3. For the sauce, fry the garlic, tomatoes and onion in a dry pan before adding about a tablespoon of water.
4. When soft, add the soy sauce and a little more water. Cook for about 10 minutes on a low heat.
5. Add the chopped basil and stir well, keep on the low heat for a further 2–4 minutes.
6. Liquidize the mixture until it is smooth and serve with the fish paté.

TIP

This dish will freeze but remember to take it out of the freezer at least 12 hours before serving and defrost it in the fridge.

CREAMY SOFT ROES WITH MUSHROOMS

Age	6–18 months
Preparation time	15 minutes
Cooking time	20 minutes
Serves	3

Soft roes make a pleasant change for a baby
and are easy to prepare. This particular dish can be a perfect weaning
food as well as a tasty snack – a very versatile item!

INGREDIENTS

8 oz (225g) soft herring roes
¼ pint (150 ml) of milk
lemon juice
2 slices bread
chopped parsley
2 oz (50g) mushrooms
salt

METHOD

1. Wash the roes and simmer gently in the milk until tender (about 10–15 minutes).
2. Remove the roes and keep the liquid (cooking liquor).
3. Blend the cooked roes with the bread, lemon juice and mushrooms in a blender, and add a little of the liquor until smooth.
4. Finally add the parsley and season with a little salt. Serve warm or cold.

TIP

You may be tempted to use the same bread that you use as a family, but remember that wholegrain or wholemeal breads may contain a little too much roughage for the very young child, so try to use fresh white bread.

GARLIC MONKFISH

Age	2 years upwards
Preparation time	10 minutes
Cooking time	see variable methods of cooking
Serves	4

INGREDIENTS

4 pieces of monkfish tail
juice of ½ lemon
2 cloves garlic (crushed)
freshly ground black pepper
chopped fresh herbs

METHOD

1. Remove any skin from the fish – a good fishmonger will do this for you on request. Wash and pat the fish dry and sprinkle with the lemon juice, crushed garlic and ground pepper. This dish can be either grilled or baked.
2. To grill, cook each side for 4–5 minutes, turning once, until the flesh near the bone is soft and white and comes away when prodded with a knife. To bake, cover and cook in a preheated hot oven (B) for 15–20 minutes
3. Serve warm sprinkled with chopped fresh parsley, a squeeze of lemon and some chopped herbs.

TIP

Monkfish has become a very popular fish recently, mainly due to its chunky, meaty texture. You can, of course, use any fish in place of monkfish, perhaps sole or plaice for younger, smaller children.

Above left: Cauliflower and courgette au gratin (page 19).

Above right: Avocado mousse with fresh lime (page 20).

Left: Sole and prawn mousse (page 22).

Above left: Banana and bacon rolls (page 26) with exotic fruit muesli (page 27).

Above right: Crêpes with scrambled eggs and smoked salmon (page 32).

Left: Face breakfast (page 35). A bacon rasher can be used in place of the sausage if preferred.

Above left: Wild mushroom soup with tarragon (page 67) and leek and potato soup (page 71).

Above right: Fillets of sole with grapes Veronique (page 76).

Left: Flakes of salmon with chive sauce (page 77).

Above left: Salmon mousse with sauce Provençale (page 78).

Above right: Sole Florentine (page 82).

Left: A plate of pasta (page 93).

Right: Fricassée of maize-fed chicken with basil flavoured tagliatelle (page 94).

Below left: Calves' liver with fresh sage and caramelized onions (page 108).

Below right: Ratatouille with brown rice (page 125).

Right: Baked bean burger with tomato sauce
(page 129).

Below left: Simple chocolate mousse (page 138) with
banana clouds (page 139).

Below right: Steven's special chocolate tart
(page 140).

Left: Strawberry syllabub (page 146), fresh pineapple cheesecake (page 148), fresh raspberry jelly (page 160) and orangesnap baskets (page 180).

Below left: Mini pizzas (page 175) and oriental style chicken (page 47) with a side dish of chipolatas.

Below right: Stefanie's birthday party table including egg heads (page 176) and Catherine wheel sandwiches (page 195).

Watermelon boats (page 187).

Stefanie enjoys a knickerbocker glory! (page 188).

Serena with her sister's birhday cake (page 189).

Wholemeal tomato quiche (page 203) and stuffed tomatoes with tuna (page 205).

SALMON MORNAY

Age	1 year upwards
Preparation time	15 minutes
Cooking time	45 minutes
Serves	2

My mother used to make this.
It is absolutely delicious but unfortunately she made it too frequently
and I remember saying 'Oh no, not salmon mornay again!' Spoiled or what!

INGREDIENTS

4 oz (110g) fresh salmon
¼ pint (150ml) milk
1 oz (25g) mild cheese
1 tomato
½ oz (12.5g) plain flour
1 oz (25g) unsalted butter
2 potatoes

METHOD

1. Make a roux, by melting the butter in a saucepan and adding the sieved flour; stir until smooth.
2. Add the milk slowly, little by little, stirring continuously with a wooden spoon.
3. When the sauce is smooth, add the cheese and stir in.
4. Cut the salmon into small pieces and poach in a little milk for 60 seconds – just enough to seal them.
5. Peel and chop the potato; boil for about 15 minutes and process until smooth.
6. Tip the salmon into a buttered, ovenproof dish and top it with the potato purée.
7. Peel, and thinly slice the tomatoes and place on top of the potato. Then pour on your thick cheesy sauce.
8. Bake in a medium preheated oven (B) for 25–30 minutes until golden brown.
9. Serve luke warm.

TIP

I always use unsalted butter for cooking for children – as well as for adults. Apart from the health aspect, salted butter can over-season your foods, without your control.

SOLE FLORENTINE

Age	1 year upwards
Preparation time	10 minutes
Cooking time	20 minutes
Serves	2

I first produced this recipe for a television programme.
They wanted something exotic and reasonably inexpensive. Serena loves
moist fish and cheese (although she wasn't always sure about the spinach) and so this
looked a relatively safe bet. Unfortunately, on the day of filming she
wasn't hungry and pushed the dish away! Don't they say something about not working
with children and animals (fish, in my case)?

INGREDIENTS

1 fillet of fresh lemon sole
1 oz (25g) mild cheese
1/4 pint (150ml) milk
1/2 oz (12.5g) fresh spinach.

METHOD

1. Remove all the skin from the fish leaving a nice clean fillet; fold it into three. Hold it together with a cocktail stick.
2. Bring the milk to the boil, and add the fish fillet. Simmer for 7 minutes.
3. Remove fish and add the spinach and cook in the milk for about 3–5 minutes.
4. Remove spinach and add the grated cheese to the milk until it becomes a fairly thickish sauce.
5. Finally serve the fish on top of the spinach and top with cheesy sauce.

TIP

Make sure that spinach leaves are well washed, at least twice washed in fact, and remove any hard stalks before cooking. Always watch your baby when she is feeding herself. If the milk evaporates add a little water.

COD FILLET WITH DILL AND BASIL

Age	1 year upwards
Preparation time	10 minutes
Cooking time	15 minutes
Serves	2

Cod is another useful fish – it is not expensive
and makes deliciously moist meals. The dill sauce accompanies it well,
especially as it has a mild flavour and does not overpower that of the fish.

INGREDIENTS

2 oz (50g) fresh cod
a squeeze of lemon
1 small onion
2 fl oz (50ml) fresh cream
1 sprig of dill (chopped)
2–3 leaves of basil (chopped)

METHOD

1. Peel and chop the onion finely and simmer it in the cream in a deep saucepan until it is soft.
2. Add the cod, cover the saucepan with tin foil and simmer for 10 minutes.
3. Chop the dill and basil. Sprinkle into the sauce and serve.
4. Serve luke warm.

TIP

Fish bones contain calcium and are therefore beneficial to children – but they hardly make the ideal ingredient! Try, therefore, to remove all the bones from the cod. If you have any doubts at all, or think some very fine small bones may remain, you can liquidize the meal before serving or force it through a fine sieve.

PLAICE WITH DUXELLE FILLING

Age	1 year upwards
Preparation time	45 minutes
Cooking time	25 minutes
Serves	4

A 'duxelle' means finely chopped mushrooms and onions.
It makes a delicious filling or topping for fish. Plaice is just one of the
many alternatives you could use.

INGREDIENTS

2 oz (50g) unsalted butter
1 oz (25g) onion
8 oz (225g) flat mushrooms
grated nutmeg
salt
fresh parsley (finely chopped)
4 large plaice fillets
1 oz (25g) flour
¼ pint (150ml) milk
lemon juice
1 tablespoon double cream
¼ pint (150ml) water

METHOD

1. Finely chop the mushrooms and onions, and remove the skin from the plaice.
2. Melt half the butter in a pan and gently fry the onion until soft and golden.
3. Add the mushrooms and cook for about 20 minutes until all the juices have evaporated and the remaining mixture is a spreadable paste.
4. Remove from the heat, season with the grated nutmeg, salt and freshly ground pepper, then transfer all but 2 tablespoons of the mixture to another bowl. Mix in 1 tablespoon of the finely chopped parsley.
5. Cut the fillets of plaice in half lengthways. Spread an equal quantity of the mushroom mixture on the skinned side of each piece.

6. Roll up the fillets from the head to the tail end and place them closely together in a baking dish.

7. Pour in ¼ pint (150ml) water and place a piece of buttered foil on top of the fish.

8. Bake in a medium preheated oven (B) for 20 minutes.

9. Melt the remaining butter in a saucepan, add the flour slowly, stir continuously and cook for 2 minutes. Remove from the heat and add the liquid from the fish slowly.

10. Add the milk and stir continuously until just before boiling point. The remaining mushroom and onion mixture should then be added.

11. Season with salt and a few drops of lemon juice. Stir in the fresh cream.

12. When the fish is cooked, transfer it to a warmed serving dish. Pour the sauce over the fish.

TIP

There are a lot of flavours in this dish, so don't over-season. Remember that nutmeg has quite a pungent flavour.

PARISIENNE OF SMOKED HADDOCK WITH TOMATO COULIS

Age	3 months upwards
Preparation time	10 minutes
Cooking time	10 minutes
Serves	2

Parisienne implies little balls or small pieces!
The haddock you choose for this dish should have the bones and skin
removed; you can do this or the fishmonger may do it for you.

INGREDIENTS

*4 oz (50g) smoked haddock
   (undyed)
1 small potato
a little vegetable purée (optional)
breadcrumbs made from 1 slice
   white bread
¼ pint (150ml) milk
unsalted butter
tomato coulis (see page 14)*

METHOD

1. Pre-cook the haddock in the milk for 5–7 minutes.
2. Purée the potatoes (see page 4).
3. Flake the haddock into small pieces and then add the potato and vegetable purées.
4. Add half of the soft white breadcrumbs (made without crusts) and a little of the cooking liquor from the haddock.
5. Roll into balls and coat with the other half of the breadcrumbs
6. Finally, fry the balls in a little unsalted butter until brown.
7. Serve with tomato coulis (see page 14).

TIP

You may prefer to substitute another fish for haddock; cod, sole, brill, turbot and bream are all suitable. You need a fish with a good texture to remain in 'chunks' during the cooking and serving but you can always add more bread to bind it firmly.

SAVOY KEDGEREE

Age	2 years upwards
Preparation time	10 minutes
Cooking time	45 minutes
Serves	3

Kedgeree is a classic dish. There are many versions but I have always enjoyed this one. I called it Savoy Kedgeree because I first learned to make it at the Savoy from this recipe.

INGREDIENTS

5 oz (140g) brown rice
¾ pint (450ml) water
salt and pepper
7 oz (200g) smoked haddock (undyed)
1 dessertspoon vegetable oil
1 onion
½ teaspoon curry powder or garam masala
2 eggs
½ pint (300ml) milk or water

METHOD

1. Place the water in a saucepan and bring to the boil. Add the rice, reduce the heat, cover and leave to simmer slowly for 30 minutes. All the water should be absorbed during this time, but if not, increase the heat.
2. Poach the fish in a mixture of milk, water and seasoning. Hard-boil the eggs.
3. Heat the oil in a non-stick frying pan, add the peeled and finely chopped onion and sauté until it begins to go golden brown. Stir in the curry powder or garam masala and cook for a further minute. Remove from the heat, add the cooked fish and keep warm.
4. Place a little rice into a serving dish and make a well in the centre. Pour in the fish and onions, garnish with finely chopped egg.

TIP

If you can't get brown rice just use standard long grain rice. Try to avoid wild rice as it is expensive and harder to the bite.

FAMILY FISH PIE

Age	1 year upwards
Preparation time	60 minutes
Cooking time	60 minutes
Serves	4–6

This dish makes a great family meal. You can feed everyone at the same time with this tasty blend of fish with cheese, cream and herbs. It is easy to cook and saves preparing various meals at dinner time.

INGREDIENTS

10 oz (275g) cod fillet
6 oz (175g) skinned haddock
7 fl oz (220ml) milk
½ bayleaf
1 oz (25g) unsalted butter
½ oz (15g) plain flour
2 tablespoons grated cheddar cheese
1 tablespoon parsley (chopped)
1 tablespoon chives (chopped)
½ tablespoon dill (chopped)
1 sliced hard boiled egg (optional)
juice of ½ lemon

FOR TOPPING

12 oz (325g) potatoes (peeled and sliced)
1 tablespoon milk
½ oz (15g) butter
1 tablespoon grated cheese

METHOD

1. Cut fish into small pieces. Bring milk and bayleaves to boil and add fish.
2. Simmer for 10 minutes.
3. While fish is cooking, cook the potatoes till soft.
4. For the topping, mash together butter and milk.
5. Drain fish (but reserve cooking liquor) and remove from pan.
6. Melt half the butter in a saucepan and add flour.
7. Cook gently then gradually add the fish liquor, simmer for 3–4 minutes.
8. Take off heat, add grated cheese and stir till smooth.
9. Fold in fish and herbs and sliced boiled egg.
10. Add lemon juice and season.
11. Mash potatoes with a little melted butter and put fish mix in baking dish topped with mashed potatoes.
12. Add a little grated cheese (for topping) to milk/butter mix (stage 4) and pour over fish pie.
13. Bake in a medium preheated oven (B) for about 20 minutes.

TIP

You can add salmon, tuna, or any fresh available fish for this dish. Serve it with a little cream and herb sauce (or similar) – see sauces – to make it nice and moist and even more tasty.

Yoghurt Quiche with Tuna Fish

Age	2 years upwards
Preparation time	50 minutes
Cooking time	45 minutes
Serves	4–6

INGREDIENTS

8 oz (225g) flour
2 oz (50g) unsalted butter
2 oz (50g) lard
3 tablespoons chilled water
salt
7 oz (200g) tuna
1 level tablespoon capers
2 eggs
5 oz (140g) natural yoghurt
salt and freshly ground pepper
1/4 oz (6g) Cheddar cheese

METHOD

1. To make the pastry, cut the butter and lard into small pieces. Rub into the flour and salt using the fingertips until the mixture resembles fine breadcrumbs. Mix in the water using a round-bladed knife.
2. Once the mixture has formed a dough, knead gently for a few seconds. Leave the pastry for 30 minutes in the fridge.
3. Roll out the pastry and line an 8 inch flan dish placed on a baking sheet. Bake in a high preheated oven (C) for 10–15 minutes.
4. Flake the tuna into a bowl. Beat the eggs and add them to the tuna. Mix in the capers and yoghurt. Season with salt and freshly ground pepper.
5. Spoon the tuna mixture into the flan case. Grate the cheese and sprinkle this over the top. Bake in a medium oven (B) for about 30 minutes. This dish can be served either hot or cold.

TIP

Using yoghurt in this recipe helps to make this quiche altogether lighter and more healthy to eat.

HOMEMADE FISH CAKES

Age   3 years upwards
Preparation time   25 minutes
Cooking time   10 minutes
Serves   4–6

Good homemade fish cakes – mmm –
you can't beat them! Once bitten forever smitten!

INGREDIENTS

1lb (450g) potatoes
*12 oz (325g) cod, haddock or other
    white fish*
1 tablespoon tomato purée
fresh chives (chopped)
2 oz (50g) wholemeal breadcrumbs
salt and pepper
a little vegetable oil

METHOD

1. Boil and mash the potatoes. Cook the fish and finely flake.
2. Mix the potatoes and fish together. Add the tomato purée, finely chopped chives and salt and pepper. Mix well until thoroughly combined.
3. Shape into 24 small flat patties, then coat with the breadcrumbs.
4. Heat a little oil in a non-stick frying pan and fry the fish cakes in 2 batches for 5 minutes, turning once.
5. Drain well on kitchen paper. The fish cakes should be served immediately, with a tomato sauce (see page 72) or something similar.

TIP

These fish cakes can be made and frozen at stage 3 of the method for a maximum of 6 months.

6
MAIN DISHES
(NON VEGETARIAN)

INTRODUCTION

I suppose this is the chapter where I have really allowed my imagination to run free. This doesn't mean that I have concocted meals that are difficult to cook or expensive to buy, but that I have cast caution aside to come up with some exciting and fresh suggestions for the young diners in your household. The meals, despite some rather grand sounding titles, are all very suitable for children, and nearly all of them would suit an adult palate too.

I have hundreds of recipes to choose from, but feel confident that the handful especially selected for this chapter truly captures the essence of my attitude towards cooking for children – that they deserve only the best. Of course, time is a major constraint, but if you do have a few spare minutes in which to prepare a meal, then give some of the following dishes a thought. They will be well worth the time.

In giving young children different meats such as turkey, guinea fowl and pheasant, and by trying them out with herbs like tarragon and sage, you are doing them a great service for later in life. They will grow up with broad tastes and an open mind to food. Because of the nature of my work, my children are trying different foods every day. But my situation is fairly exceptional; most families, not surprisingly, tend to use a smaller range of ingredients in their cooking than I do.

It is a shame when children grow up believing that they dislike certain foods. Although I try not to show it, I do become frustrated if children tell me that they don't like something when I know that they have never tried it. I don't take it personally, and plenty of adults have been just as difficult, but perhaps they are denying themselves something they would really enjoy.

A final point to make concerns the ingredients. For each recipe I have provided a complete list of necessary items. As some of the meals in this chapter are a little complicated, the lists are necessarily longer. Don't be put off if you find you have something missing. Remember, these are ideas prepared *à la* Steven Saunders; you don't have to follow the recipe to the letter. Try out some ideas of your own: vary the spices, or even the main ingredient. Serve the dish in a slightly different way, or change the quantities involved.

Pasta (for Noodles)

Age	6 months upwards
Preparation time	1 hour 10 minutes
Cooking time	5 minutes
Serves	2

Making pasta is really not as difficult as you may think.
I have included it here, not only as an accompaniment to many of the
main meals I am recommending, but also as a meal suggestion in its own right. Simply
make up some pasta and use it with any sauce you have to hand – both
the texture and taste are plain and smooth, and therefore it is ideal for children who may
be a little bit picky about what they eat.

INGREDIENTS

9 oz (250g) plain flour
2 whole eggs and 1 egg yolk
salt

METHOD

1. Put the eggs and flour with a pinch of salt and 4 tablespoonfuls of water in a food processor. Mix for about 30 seconds until well blended.
2. Remove the mixture and knead until you produce a perfectly smooth dough.
3. Wrap in film and keep in the fridge for 1 hour.
4. Now the difficult bit ... Cut the rested dough into four or five pieces and place on a lightly floured surface. Roll out as thin as possible, from the centre each time. Cut into thin strips.
5. For cooking, place in boiling buttered water for 2–3 minutes; the time will depend upon the thickness you have achieved.

TIP

A pasta machine is not essential – but neither is it expensive. It may be well worth buying one if you enjoy the taste of your own pasta. And don't forget, fresh pasta freezes well and can also be flavoured with spices, herbs and vegetables.

FRICASSÉE OF MAIZE-FED CHICKEN WITH BASIL FLAVOURED TAGLIATELLE

Age	1 year upwards
Preparation time	15 minutes
Cooking time	35 minutes
Serves	6

A classic dish, both rich and delicious.
It serves to illustrate many of the points I was making in the introduction,
not least the concept of giving your children the best. Please note, before you begin, that
the saucepan used in stage 1 has to be transferred to the oven later, so
you must choose one which is suitable.

INGREDIENTS

1 ×3lb (1350g) chicken
unsalted butter
2 oz (50g) mushrooms
½ pint (300ml) of double cream
½ clove garlic
fresh parsley
3–4 leaves of fresh basil
½ pint (300ml) of chicken stock

METHOD

1. Bone and joint the chicken. Chop the garlic and fry (in a heavy, oven-usable saucepan) with the chicken in a little unsalted butter for about 5 minutes.
2. Put the saucepan in a low, preheated oven (A) for 20 minutes.
3. Remove the pan from the oven, add the chicken stock and then reduce by half (either in the oven or on the hob).
4. Slice the mushrooms, and chop the parsley and basil. Add these ingredients to the pan with the cream. Cook for about a further 10 minutes.
5. Finally, remove some of the chicken from the bone and serve with some of the sauce and fresh pasta.

TIP

It's worth saying a quick word about the possibility of salmonella poisoning. Avoid all risk by cooking the chicken thoroughly. Complete defrosting is also important if you have used frozen chicken.

LAMBS' LIVER CASSEROLE

Age	1 year upwards
Preparation time	25 minutes
Cooking time	35 minutes
Serves	6

I have to say honestly 'it's not one of my favourites'.
I don't like liver or beans very much but thankfully my children do! This
is one that Daddy definitely doesn't delve into!

INGREDIENTS

12 oz (325g) lambs' liver
1 oz (25g) flour
1 oz (25g) unsalted butter
1 small onion
4 oz (100g) mushrooms
medium-sized can red kidney beans
¼ pint (150ml) beef stock
¼ pint (150ml) milk
2 level tablespoons tomato purée
1 level teaspoon dried mixed herbs
salt
freshly ground pepper

METHOD

1. Finely chopped the onions and slice the mushrooms. Cut the liver into small cubes, roll them in flour, and fry these three ingredients in the butter in a large saucepan. The frying should be brisk, until the ingredients are light brown.
2. Add the beans to the liver mixture and stir in before adding all the other ingredients.
3. Bring this to the boil and simmer for 20–25 minutes.
4. Serve hot with rice or potatoes.

TIP

You can replace kidney beans with any type of haricot bean or even tinned baked beans for simplicity; and you can use lambs' kidneys if you prefer, instead of liver.

WHOLEWHEAT PASTA AND TUNA FISH CASSEROLE

Age	3 years upwards
Preparation time	15 minutes
Cooking time	20 minutes
Serves	4

INGREDIENTS

2 carrots
2 celery sticks
4 oz (100g) frozen peas
6 oz (175g) dried wholewheat pasta
2 tablespoons oil
1 onion
2 tablespoons plain wholemeal flour
½ pint (300ml) milk
7 oz (200g) fresh tuna
4 oz (100g) Cheddar cheese
3 tablespoons wholemeal breadcrumbs

METHOD

1. Slice the carrots and celery into a saucepan, cover with cold water and bring to the boil.
2. Cover and cook for 15 minutes, adding the peas for the last 5 minutes. Drain, reserving the liquid, and set aside.
3. Cook the pasta; drain and set aside.
4. Chop the onion and fry until soft in the oil. Remove from the heat and stir in the flour.
5. Make up the reserved liquid to about ¾ pint (450ml) with some milk. Gradually add this to the pan, stirring constantly until blended.
6. Bring to the boil and cook for 3 minutes; it should be moderately thick.
7. Grate the cheese and flake the tuna. Add the tuna and half the cheese together with the carrots, celery, peas and pasta to the sauce.
8. Turn into a shallow ovenproof dish. Sprinkle the remaining cheese and breadcrumbs over the top.
9. Cook under a preheated hot grill for 3–4 minutes, until golden brown and bubbling. Serve immediately.

TIP

I buy fresh tuna for my restaurant. Recently, I have seen it in many supermarkets – if you can get it, do! And also ... try to use fresh pasta.

GOUJONS OF TURKEY FILLET WITH A GARLIC CRUST

Age	1 year upwards
Preparation time	10 minutes
Cooking time	10 minutes
Serves	3

I use garlic quite a lot for young children.
Mine enjoy the taste, providing it is in moderation. I suspect that some
parents might tell their children that they won't like garlic, but I treat it like any other herb
and use it where I consider it can add a new dimension to what might
otherwise be a bland taste.

INGREDIENTS

8 oz (225g) turkey fillets
3 tablespoons of white
   breadcrumbs
1 egg
3 tablespoons plain flour
2 garlic cloves
parsley
salt
a little milk

METHOD

1. Crush the garlic and add this to the egg which should be lightly beaten with a little milk.
2. Chop the parsley and mix with the flour and a pinch of salt.
3. Cut the turkey into thin strips and dip each into the flour and chopped parsley mix, then the egg and garlic mix.
4. Then dip the turkey in the breadcrumbs.
5. Place on a greased baking tray and bake in a high pre-heated oven (C) for 15 minutes.

TIP

Serve with either a tomato or fresh herb sauce on the side (see sauces in Chapter 4).

GUINEA FOWL WITH BANANA CASSEROLE SCENTED WITH TARRAGON

Age	1 year upwards
Preparation time	15 minutes
Cooking time	25 minutes
Serves	4

Guinea fowl can be likened to chicken.
It is now farmed and so availability and price are more stable and of similar cost to chicken. This is a distinctly savoury dish, although the bananas sweeten it a little, which will appeal to the child's palate. It was always very popular.

INGREDIENTS

1 small guinea fowl
1 sprig of tarragon (optional)
2 bananas
½ pint (300ml) of chicken stock
½ pint (300ml) of cream or natural yoghurt
1 small onion
1 carrot
1 celery stick
1 bayleaf
salt
a small amount of unsalted butter
dash of olive oil

METHOD

1. Chop the onion finely and fry for few minutes in the butter with a dash of olive oil.
2. Add the jointed guinea fowl and seal by frying for 3 minutes; colour each side a little only.
3. Slice the vegetables and add these and the bayleaf to the guinea fowl.
4. Add the stock and a little salt and bring to boiling point before reducing the heat and simmering for 15 minutes.
5. Add the cream or yoghurt and stir in well before taking out the guinea fowl joints and removing the flesh from the bone.
6. Reduce the sauce on a high heat for about 10 minutes or until the cream thickens.
7. Finally add the chopped tarragon leaves and the slices of banana before reheating and serving as a sauce with the guinea fowl.

TIP

Allow the sauce to cool considerably before serving. This will help it to thicken even more. If you use natural yoghurt instead of cream it should be the very last thing you add, and don't use a high heat once the yoghurt has been added.

ESCALOPE OF TURKEY BREAST 'FINES HERBS'

Age	1 year upwards
Preparation time	15 minutes
Cooking time	10 minutes
Serves	1

INGREDIENTS

*8 oz (225g) turkey fillet ½ inch
   thick*
3 tablespoons wholemeal flour
1 egg
2 tablespoons milk
wholemeal breadcrumbs
freshly ground white pepper
fresh parsley (chopped)
fresh herbs (chopped)
1 tablespoon ground coriander

METHOD

1. Remove the skin and cut the turkey into thin slices.
2. Season the flour with the herbs and pepper and gently beat the egg with about 2 tablespoonfuls of milk.
3. Dip each turkey slice into the flour and then dip into the egg mixture; finally, roll in the breadcrumbs.
4. Place on a greased baking tray and bake in a preheated hot oven (C) for 10 minutes.

TIP

This is particularly nice served with a warm fresh tomato and basil sauce (see page 72).

CITRUS CHICKEN

Age	3 months upwards
Preparation time	15 minutes
Cooking time	1 hour 20 minutes
Serves	4

INGREDIENTS

1 carrot
1 celery stick
1 onion
1 bayleaf
juice of 1 lemon
1 pint (575ml) chicken stock
1 small chicken
1 level tablespoon arrowroot
freshly ground salt and pepper
4 tablespoons plain yoghurt
chopped tarragon

METHOD

1. Scrub and thinly slice the carrot and celery, and peel and slice the onion. Add to the bayleaf, lemon juice and about 1 pint of chicken stock in a large saucepan and bring to the boil.

2. Skin and joint the chicken into 8 pieces. Place the chicken in the liquid and cover and simmer for at least 45 minutes. Check that it is thoroughly cooked by piercing the thickest parts with a skewer – there should be no pink juices left at all. Remove the chicken and keep warm.

3. When the chicken is ready, boil the stock to reduce it by half, to ½ pint, to strengthen the flavour. Strain and discard the vegetables.

4. Pour the reduced stock into a saucepan. Blend in the arrowroot to a smooth paste with a little water.

5. Bring to the boil, stirring occasionally, then simmer for 10 minutes, or until the sauce thickens. Add seasoning to taste. Add a little more lemon juice if required, and the chopped tarragon.

6. Arrange the chicken pieces on a serving dish, and pour over the sauce and yoghurt.

TIP

If you are a bit unsure about cutting up chicken, ask your butcher to do it for you, or alternatively, buy 8 separate chicken pieces.

BREAST OF PHEASANT WITH CITRUS SAUCE

Age	1 year upwards
Preparation time	15 minutes
Cooking time	25 minutes
Serves	2

In season, pheasant is deliciously fresh and tender. However, ensure that the bird you choose has not been too well hung, especially for children; it is the hanging that strengthens the flavour. Chicken or turkey also work well if pheasant is unavailable, but when it is in season it is usually fairly cheap.

INGREDIENTS

1 spring onion
1 carrot
1 breast of pheasant (off the bone)
2 oranges
1 lemon
¼ pint (150ml) chicken stock
¼ pint (150ml) of double cream
salt
unsalted butter
olive oil

METHOD

1. Slice the carrot lengthwise and finely chop the spring onion. Fry these in a little butter with a dash of olive oil until tender.
2. Slice the breast of pheasant into ¼ × 2-inch strips and seal in the pan with the vegetables.
3. Add the chicken stock and reduce by half; this should take about 5 minutes on a high heat.
4. Remove the pieces of pheasant and set aside.
5. To the sauce, add the juice of the lemon and oranges.
6. Gradually add the cream, heat through to thicken, reduce and add salt to taste.
7. Finally, put the pheasant back into the sauce and heat 2–3 more minutes.

TIP

With many meals which end with the dish being heated, it is important to leave a little time for it to cool. This improves the flavour and, of course, prevents children from burning their tongues!

LAMBS' KIDNEY ORIENTAL

Age	1 year upwards
Preparation time	5 minutes
Cooking time	10 minutes
Serves	1

If your baby were to choose her own food
she would probably pass this recipe over. However, she may be converted,
and would definitely benefit. Kidneys are loaded with protein, vitamins and iron.

INGREDIENTS

1 lamb's kidney
3 teaspoons of smooth peanut
  butter
1 teaspoon of honey
2 tablespoons cow's milk
unsalted butter

METHOD

1. Ask your butcher to remove the membrane that surrounds the kidney and to halve it so he can snip off the core in the centre.
2. Slice the kidney into ½ inch cubes and gently fry in a pan with a little unsalted butter for about 3 minutes each side.
3. Add 2 tablespoonfuls of milk and simmer for 2–3 minutes.
4. Add the peanut butter and honey and blend in.
5. Taste the sauce and check the kidney is not pink and serve luke warm.

TIP

Although it is suggested that you ask your butcher to prepare the kidney, it is very simple to do yourself. Use a sharp knife; the membrane (if any exists) and the sinews are easy to identify and remove. And because kidneys are so good for your baby, try to serve the meat at least once every week. Make sure you cook the kidneys well – not pink.

RAGOÛT OF BEEF (NORMANDY)

Age	1 year upwards
Preparation time	15 minutes
Cooking time	1 hour 15 minutes
Serves	2

A ragoût is a beef stew,
although you can make this with lamb instead . . . and call it a navarin.
This ragoût is described as Normandy style because it contains apples. You will find that
this is one of the tastiest of the meals for the very young, so the persuasive
game of 'one for you and one for me' takes on a new meaning.

INGREDIENTS

2–3 oz (50–75g) of lean stewing
    beef
1 small potato
1 small apple
4 fl oz (100ml) cow's milk
1 slice of wholemeal bread
unsalted butter

METHOD

1. Make sure all the fat is removed from the meat and then cut into ½ inch cubes.
2. Seal the meat by turning briefly in a little hot unsalted butter.
3. Add the milk and simmer for about 45 minutes. You may need to add more milk if the pan starts to look dry.
4. Chop the bread and add to the meat after 40 minutes of simmering.
5. Peel and cube the potato (½ inch cubes) and boil for 15 minutes.
6. Peel and core the apple; add to the potato and cook for a further 5–7 minutes.
7. Blend the beef with the potato and apple mix until smooth and serve luke warm.

TIP

Save a little of the juice from cooking the potato and apple to add to the final purée if it looks too dry.

SPICY SPAGHETTI (MILLIGETTI)

Age	2 years upwards
Preparation time	15 minutes
Cooking time	35 minutes
Serves	4

INGREDIENTS

1 tablespoon oil
1 onion
1 clove garlic
8 oz (225g) minced beef
1 tablespoon flour
2 oz (25g) bulgur wheat
14 oz (375g) can tomatoes
1 tablespoon tomato purée
1 tablespoon soy sauce
½ pint (300ml) vegetable stock
salt and pepper
Parmesan cheese

METHOD

1. Chop the onion and fry in the oil until softened. Add the crushed garlic and beef and cook, stirring so that the meat is broken up as it seals. Remove from the heat, drain off any fat, then stir in the flour.

2. Add the remaining ingredients, except the cheese, bring to the boil, then cover and simmer for 35 minutes, until cooked.

3. Cook the spaghetti (or fresh pasta rolls) till soft (but not mushy) and serve the meat poured over the pasta.

TIP

This is best eaten with fresh spaghetti.

VEGGIE BAKE

Age	2 years upwards
Preparation time	20 minutes
Cooking time	1 hour 40 minutes
Serves	4

Although I have made this with tomatoes and potatoes
you can, of course, add any vegetables you like and top in the same way
with the potato.

INGREDIENTS

1 tablespoon oil
1 onion
1 clove of garlic
8 oz (225g) minced beef
1 tablespoon flour
2 oz (50g) millet or bulgur wheat
14 oz (375g) tin of tomatoes
1 tablespoon tomato purée
1 tablespoon soy sauce
½ pint (300ml) vegetable stock
4 fresh tomatoes
4 tablespoons tomato sauce
1 lb (450g) potatoes
oil for brushing

METHOD

1. Finely chop the onion and fry in the oil until softened. Add the crushed garlic and beef and cook well. Remove from the heat and drain off any excess fat. Stir in the flour; this is Milligetti (see page 105).
2. Add the millet or bulgur wheat, tin of tomatoes, tomato purée, soy sauce and vegetable stock and bring to the boil. Cover and simmer for 35 minutes.
3. Boil and then slice the potatoes.
4. Using 4 individual ovenproof dishes, divide up the mixture. Skin and slice the tomatoes and arrange them on top. Then spread tomato sauce over each one.
5. Arrange the potatoes in overlapping slices on top of each dish, brush lightly with oil and cook in a high preheated oven (C) for 30 minutes, until lightly browned. These should be served hot.

TIP

A good vegetarian dish as well. Just omit the beef and add plenty of fresh, seasonal vegetables.

CASSEROLE OF BEEF AND VEGETABLES WITH A SHALLOT SAUCE

Age	1 year upwards
Preparation time	15 minutes
Cooking time	2 hours
Serves	6 (or 2 adults and 2–3 children)

This is an ideal family meal, enjoyed by everyone.
You can add red wine to your portion if you like, for a more adult flavour.

INGREDIENTS

12 oz (325g) of lean braising steak
1 small onion or 2 shallots
1 small bunch of baby carrots
4 baby turnips
4 baby squash (or courgettes)
4 whole mushrooms
4 baby sweetcorns
1 glass red wine
1 pint (565ml) beef stock
1 bayleaf
fresh parsley (chopped)
1 tablespoon of tomato purée
unsalted butter
olive oil
salt

METHOD

1. Wash and trim the vegetables, but leave them whole.
2. Cut the beef into 1 inch cubes and fry with the vegetables (except the mushrooms) and bayleaf in a little butter and olive oil until the beef is slightly brown.
3. Add the tomato purée and stir on the heat for 2–3 minutes.
4. Add the stock and the red wine, bring to the boil and reduce well.
5. Add a little salt to taste and simmer for about 2 hours. Alternatively place in warm oven (A) for about the same length of time.
6. Lastly, slice the mushrooms and cook for a final 5 minutes before allowing to cool, topping with parsley and serving.

TIP

You can speed up this recipe by tenderizing the meat by pounding it well before cooking, although the dish does benefit from slow cooking. The rich, succulent flavour is retained if kept in a tight container in the fridge for a few days, or in the freezer for up to 6 months.

CALVES' LIVER WITH FRESH SAGE AND CARAMELIZED ONIONS

Age	6 months upwards
Preparation time	15 minutes
Cooking time	25 minutes
Serves	2

This recipe is nutritious and versatile.
Not only does it utilize iron and protein-rich liver, but it can be both
served as here or puréed for younger children. I find it a good way of introducing children
to onion as they sometimes *think* they dislike the texture and taste.

INGREDIENTS

¼ onion
2 oz (50g) unsalted butter
1 teaspoon of olive oil
1 calf's liver
fresh chervil
1 teaspoon of honey
2 fl oz (50ml) of chicken stock
tomato purée

METHOD

1. Peel and slice the onion into small, thin slices and place in a thick, flat-bottomed saucepan with half the butter (melted) and the oil.
2. Cook for about 15 minutes, stirring continuously.
3. Reduce the chicken stock by at least half in a separate pan, then add the honey.
4. Finely chop the fresh chervil and reserve for later.
5. Cut the liver into strips and seal in the rest of the butter (heated with a dash of oil) in a frying pan for 5 minutes, stirring continuously.
6. Meanwhile, add the onion mixture and tomato purée to the simmering stock and bring to the boil, stirring. Skim if necessary.
8. Finally add the chervil to the sauce. Pour the sauce over the liver in the frying pan and then serve at a warm temperature.

TIP

You can elect to replace calves' liver with chicken liver – which is cheaper – or even duck livers.

Lamb Tikka Kebabs

Age	3 years upwards
Preparation time	15 minutes
Cooking time	8 minutes
Serves	4

I love Indian food and spices.
People always frown when I mention that occasionally I like to cook
an Indian meal for my children. You'd be amazed how they enjoy it as long as it is not too
spicy. These kebabs have a slightly spicy flavour and they can also be
barbecued very successfully.

INGREDIENTS

1 tablespoon oil
1 clove garlic
1 teaspoon tandoori spice mix
4 tablespoons natural yoghurt
1 tablespoon lemon juice
12 oz (325g) lean lamb (or chicken)
1 red pepper
2 small onions

FRIED RICE

1 tablespoon oil
1 onion
12 oz (325g) cooked brown rice
*7 oz (200g) can sweetcorn kernels
  (optional)*
1 tablespoon parsley (chopped)

METHOD

1. Remove any excess fat and cut the meat into 1 inch cubes.
2. Mix together the oil, garlic, spice, yoghurt and lemon juice. Add the meat and stir until well coated.
3. Core and seed the pepper and cut into squares, cut 1 onion into 8 pieces.
4. Using 4 large skewers, thread on alternate pieces of meat, red pepper and onion. Cook under a medium grill for 8 minutes, turning frequently.
5. To make fried rice: chop the onion and fry in oil until softened. Add the remaining ingredients and stir constantly until heated through.
6. Serve the kebabs with the rice.

TIP

To make the overall flavour milder, serve with a tomato sauce blended with a little cream and some of the juices from the kebab.

BEEF AND CORIANDER SAUSAGES

Age	3 years upwards
Preparation time	20 minutes
Cooking time	8–10 minutes
Serves	4–6

I like to make my own sausages,
you can't beat them, especially when you know the secret of the tasty
ingredients!

INGREDIENTS

4 oz ((100g) wholemeal
    breadcrumbs
4 tablespoons water
8 oz (225g) lean minced beef
1 small onion
1 clove garlic
1 egg yolk
2 tablespoons tomato purée
1 teaspoon paprika
1 teaspoon ground coriander
plain wholemeal flour for coating
salt and pepper

METHOD

1. Place the breadcrumbs in a bowl, pour over about 4 tablespoons of water and mix together. Add the remaining ingredients and mix thoroughly with your hands.
2. Divide the mixture into 12 portions and, with still wet hands, roll each portion into a 4 inch long, thin sausage shape.
3. Roll the sausages in the flour and coat evenly.
4. Cook under a preheated hot grill for 8–10 minutes, turning occasionally.

TIP

Serve with tomato sauce, mashed potato and a vegetable accompaniment, or in pitta bread with salad.

7
MAIN MEALS
(VEGETARIAN)

INTRODUCTION

For the purposes of this chapter, and indeed the whole book, I have classified as vegetarian any meal that doesn't contain meat (or meat products) or fish (or fish products). I know that some people consider themselves vegetarian and yet still eat a little white fish.

I am not a vegetarian, but understand and appreciate the reasons why people decide to stop eating meat and fish. Personally, I have never considered becoming vegetarian. My job would make it virtually impossible, and, anyway, I don't think I could manage without the occasional breast of pheasant or slice of lamb. Having said that, we do often have 'vegetarian days' at home which always leave us feeling healthy and refreshed. And we do, of course, serve vegetarian dishes at the restaurant, so I know that vegetarian meals can be both tasty and nutritious.

The ideas in this chapter, as elsewhere, are based on the basic principles of fresh foods and healthy cooking. Children think less about the ingredients of meals, more about the taste and appearance. They are unlikely to complain if something doesn't contain meat. Indeed, in my experience, many young children go through a stage of wanting to be vegetarian . . . a stage they quickly forget if encouraged to.

Anyway, here are a few ideas. And like most of the recipes in the book, they are not just for the kids . . . baked bean burgers in particular.

LENTIL SHEPHERD'S PIE

Age	9 months upwards
Preparation time	15 minutes
Cooking time	2 hours
Serves	4

This is a dish to give to non-vegetarians
who believe that you need meat to make a meal tasty and complete.
They will probably never question the ingredients of this wholesome and filling shepherd's
pie, but simply enjoy the rich tastes of what is one of my personal favourites
for a winter's evening. And remember, before you start this one, the lentils need to be
washed and then soaked for 8 hours before use.

INGREDIENTS

8 oz (225g) yellow or green lentils
1 pint (575ml) of vegetable stock
2 large tomatoes (tinned plum or
    fresh)
1 medium-sized onion
1 clove of garlic
2 carrots
2 sticks of celery
4 oz (100g) field mushrooms (or
    button mushrooms)
fresh nutmeg
dried thyme, tarragon, marjoram
    or similar herbs
1 red pepper
1 tablespoon of vegetable oil

FOR THE TOPPING

2 lbs (900g) potatoes
3 fl oz (75ml) milk
1 oz (25g) mild cheese

METHOD

1. Drain the lentils, which should have been previously soaked in water for about 8 hours, and place in a saucepan with the vegetable stock. Boil for 1 hour.
2. Prepare the vegetables by peeling and chopping the onions and carrots. Finely slice the celery, mushrooms and tomatoes and crush the garlic. The pepper needs to be deseeded and sliced. Grate the nutmeg until you have about ¼ teaspoon. The potatoes for the topping need peeling and scrubbing.
3. Heat the vegetable oil in a saucepan and add the onions, carrots, garlic, celery and pepper. Fry for 10 minutes until the vegetables soften.
4. Add the sliced mushrooms and cook for a further 1 minute.
5. Mix the vegetables in with the stock and lentils and add the tomatoes, a pinch of your chosen herbs and the nutmeg.
6. Turn this mixture into an ovenproof dish.

7. The potatoes need slicing and boiling for about 25 minutes or until slightly softer than for normal eating. Then mash them with the milk and half the cheese. Make them quite creamy.

8. Spread the potatoes over the mixture, top with the remainder of the cheese and bake in a low preheated oven (A) for about 20 minutes or until golden brown.

TIP

Don't worry about doing certain things in this recipe that I'm generally opposed to, for example, use tinned tomatoes if you want.

VEGETABLE GRATIN

Age	2 years upwards
Preparation time	10 minutes
Cooking time	15–20 minutes
Serves	2

Gratin means to glaze under a hot grill usually with cheese.

INGREDIENTS

3 oz (75g) broccoli
3 oz (75g) cauliflower florets
1 carrot
2 oz (50g) peas
1 oz (25g) unsalted butter
3 tablespoons plain wholemeal
 flour
6 fl oz (200ml) milk
2 oz (50g) Cheddar cheese
2 tablespoons wholemeal
 breadcrumbs
1 teaspoon sesame seeds
salt and pepper

METHOD

1. Thinly slice the carrot and cook with the cauliflower and broccoli in boiling water for 8 minutes. Add the peas and cook for a further 4 minutes. Drain and keep warm.
2. Melt the butter in a pan, remove from the heat and stir in the flour. Blend in the milk, and salt and pepper, return to the heat and bring to the boil, stirring constantly.
3. Grate the cheese and add half to the sauce together with the cooked vegetables.
4. Turn into a large shallow ovenproof dish and sprinkle with the breadcrumbs, remaining cheese and sesame seeds.
5. Place under a preheated hot grill for a few minutes, until golden brown and bubbling. Serve immediately.

ORIENTAL SPINACH

Age	1 year upwards
Preparation time	5 minutes
Cooking time	10 minutes
Serves	3

INGREDIENTS

1 oz (25g) sesame seeds
8 oz (225g) fresh spinach leaves
1 tablespoon soy sauce
1 teaspoon sugar
3 tablespoons water

METHOD

1. Sprinkle the sesame seeds into a deep frying pan and heat, moving them around constantly until they turn a pale golden colour.
2. Meanwhile, carefully wash the spinach and remove the coarse stalks. Cook it in a small amount of water for 2 minutes.
3. When cooked, press out any water by squeezing with the back of a large spoon.
4. Crush the seeds in a processor (reserving a few to sprinkle over the spinach) and they will become a fine powder.
5. Mix the powder with the soy sauce, sugar and water until it reaches a creamy consistency.
6. Roughly chop the spinach, pour over the sesame sauce and sprinkle with the toasted whole sesame seeds.

TIP

This sesame sauce can be used for other vegetable and meat dishes.

CARROT MOUSSELINE (ENCASED IN LEEK LEAVES)

Age	9 months upwards
Preparation time	25 minutes
Cooking time	30 minutes
Serves	3

Exotic sounding dishes that are relatively easy
to prepare are always favourites with me. This dish scores not only with
its taste but also with its appearance – and yet is simple to make. And like many of these
vegetarian meal ideas, carrot mousseline is equally suitable for adults.
The leek case is optional, and perhaps best omitted for very young children.

INGREDIENTS

2 medium-sized carrots
½ pint (300ml) fresh orange juice
2 fl oz (50ml) double cream
4 egg yolks (depending on size)
salt
the inner leaves of 1–2 leeks

METHOD

1. Clean and chop the carrots before boiling them to a pulp in the orange juice.
2. Add the double cream, stir well and reduce.
3. Blend in a liquidizer until very smooth.
4. Add the egg yolks and a little salt and mix well. This is the mousseline.
5. To encase the mousseline, wash thoroughly the inner leaves of a split leek. Boil until soft and line 3 buttered ramekins (or individual ovenproof dishes) with the leaves, allowing enough height to fold in and over the mousseline.

6. Pour the mousseline into the ramekins and encase by folding the tops of the leek leaves over. Poach by placing in a saucepan with boiling water, which should come about halfway up the ramekin for 15–20 minutes. Do not allow to boil dry.

7. To serve, ideally with a selection of vegetables, turn out the encased mousseline onto a warm plate.

TIP

The encasement does take up time and trouble, but it is well worth it in terms of appearance and taste. The mousseline can be served along with a selection of vegetables, or it is equally as nice with a sauce.

BABY BROAD BEANS WITH PARSLEY AND LEMON

Age	2 years upwards
Preparation time	10 minutes
Cooking time	20 minutes
Serves	6

I love the flavour of the first freshly picked broad beans of the year. Prepared in this simple way, they make not only a good vegetable dish, but a good main dish as well.

INGREDIENTS

4 lb (2kg) broad beans
2 oz (50g) unsalted butter
5 level tablespoons flour
¾ pint (450ml) vegetable stock
salt and freshly ground pepper
2 egg yolks
6 tablespoons single cream
3 tablespoons fresh parsley
    (chopped)
2 tablespoons lemon juice

METHOD

1. Shell and thoroughly wash the beans. Cook in a pan of boiling water for about 15 minutes until tender. Drain and place in a covered vegetable dish to keep warm.
2. For the sauce, melt the butter in a pan, stir in the flour and cook gently for 1 minute, stirring continuously. Remove from the heat and slowly stir in the stock.
3. Bring to the boil, and continue to stir until the sauce thickens. Add seasoning and simmer for about 5 minutes.
4. Beat the egg yolks with the fresh cream, add about 6 tablespoonfuls of the hot sauce and mix well.
5. Remove the pan from the heat, add the egg mixture and stir. Cook over a low heat until the sauce thickens a little more.
6. Remove from the heat and stir in the chopped parsley and lemon juice. Season to taste and pour over the broad beans.

TIP

If you can get baby broad beans, they are even more tender and delicious – the delicate flavour is lost if the beans are old and tough. You can substitute broad beans with other vegetables if preferred.

FROMAGE FRAIS BAKERS

Age	2 years upwards
Preparation time	10 minutes
Cooking time	1 hour 30 minutes
Serves	4

Baked potatoes make an extremely good meal
with an endless variety of fillings. This is just one way of serving this
popular dish.

INGREDIENTS

2 large potatoes
4 oz (100g) Cheddar cheese
4 spring onions
3 tablespoons fromage frais
salt and pepper

METHOD

1. Wash and dry the potatoes and make a long slit along one side of each. Bake in a hot preheated oven (C) for $1\frac{1}{4}$ hours or until cooked.
2. Halve the potatoes lengthways, scoop out the flesh into a bowl.
3. Grate the cheese and mash this with the flesh from the potatoes.
4. Chop the spring onions and add these to the potato mixture together with the fromage frais. Mix until well blended.
5. Season with salt and pepper.
6. Spoon the mixture into the potato skins, sprinkle with the remaining cheese and return to the oven until they turn a golden brown colour.
7. Serve with a salad.

TIP

Two delicious variations are sweetcorn potatoes (omit the spring onions and mix 4 oz (100g) cooked sweetcorn with the potato) and baked bean potatoes (blend the baked beans in with the fromage frais).

FRESH BEANS ON TOAST

Age	3 years upwards
Preparation time	5 minutes
Cooking time	50 minutes
Serves	4

Pinto beans are just one variety
of the many dried beans you can get on the market. If you can't get hold
of them, try mung, haricot or even flagoulet beans.

INGREDIENTS

8 oz (225g) pinto beans
pinch of salt
1 dessertspoon of tomato purée
1 teaspoon Dijon mustard
1 clove puréed garlic
3 fl oz (75ml) pure apple juice
½ teaspoon Worcestershire sauce
1 bayleaf

METHOD

1. Soak the beans overnight and then drain well.
2. Place in cold water to cover and boil rapidly for 10 minutes with the bayleaf. Cover and simmer gently for 25 minutes, adding the salt towards the end of cooking time.
3. Drain well and return to the pan adding the remaining ingredients.
4. Bring to the boil, cover and simmer gently for 15 minutes. Discard the bayleaf.
5. The beans should be served hot, with wholemeal toast and grated cheese glazed on top if you wish.

TIP

This recipe can be simplified by using tinned baked beans instead!

CASSATA

Age	2 years upwards
Preparation time	20 minutes (plus 3 hours freezing)
Serves	6

Cassata is a cream based sweet that has hundreds of variations. This version combines fruits and nuts and is therefore better for older children. With so much sweetness already in the recipe, nuts make a good contrast of flavour.

INGREDIENTS

½ pint (300ml) double cream
3 oz (90g) sugar
1 egg white
2½oz (70g) candied, diced fruits
1 oz (30g) pistachio nuts
1 oz (30g) hazelnuts

METHOD

1. Make sure that the nuts are cleaned and finely chopped.
2. Whip the cream until stiff and then refrigerate.
3. Heat the sugar in a little water until the consistency of syrup.
4. Whisk the egg white and add to the still warm sugar; whisk continuously until the mixture has cooled.
5. Add the fruits and nuts and fold in the cream.
6. The mixture should then be frozen for 3 hours and served in slices, ideally with a fruit sauce.

TIP

For the above, try a simple raspberry sauce: fresh raspberries squeezed through a fine sieve.

CREAMY MUSHROOMS

Age	3 months upwards
Preparation time	5 minutes
Cooking time	25 minutes
Serves	4

This is one of those recipes
which is probably thought of as a side vegetable for adults, but which
makes an excellent meal, on its own, for children. If you are going to serve it in
conjunction with other foods, then try it with chicken or fish.

INGREDIENTS

*½ square inch of fresh ginger
    (finely chopped)
1 clove garlic (crushed)
2 oz (50g) mushrooms
1 oz (25g) unsalted butter
¼ pint (150ml) fresh double cream
fresh tarragon (chopped)*

METHOD

1. Wipe and slice the mushrooms and then fry them in the butter with the garlic and ginger.
2. Add the cream and reduce when thick. Add the tarragon and serve warm.

TIP

You don't need to limit this recipe – try carrots, celeriac and even broad beans.

SPICY CHEESE AND TOMATO DIP

Age	6 months upwards
Preparation time	15 minutes
Cooking time	none
Serves	6

Please don't be put off by the word 'spicy'
since paprika pepper isn't really hot. It simply adds a nice zest to the
dish which children find enjoyable.

INGREDIENTS

4 oz (100g) Cheshire cheese
   (grated)
2 oz (50g) unsalted butter
1 small onion
1 level teaspoon mustard powder
1 tablespoon tomato ketchup
2 tablespoons fresh single cream
Worcestershire sauce
paprika pepper
fresh parsley to garnish

METHOD

1. Soften the butter and beat this together in a bowl with the cheese, using a wooden spoon.
2. Grate the onion directly into the mixture and add the mustard powder, tomato ketchup, fresh cream and a little Worcestershire sauce. Season with a dash of paprika pepper and mix well.
3. Place the dip in a fresh bowl and garnish with a parsley sprig.

TIP

Serve this with raw vegetables (crudités), cheese biscuits or bread sticks as a snack, or even warmed slightly as a sauce for use with another dish.

PASTA WITH PESTO SAUCE

Age	6 months upwards
Preparation time	10 minutes
Cooking time	10 minutes
Serves	3

You can make noodles in different shapes,
not just long thin strips. Children sometimes find snakey noodles fun,
or try individual raviolis with various fillings.

INGREDIENTS

12 oz (325g) fresh pasta
2 oz (50g) fresh basil
1 clove garlic
2 tablespoons of olive oil
1 tablespoon of pine nuts
2 tablespoons of Parmesan cheese
   (grated)
a little unsalted butter
hot water

METHOD

1. Follow the recipe for fresh pasta as on page 93.
2. Put the basil, peeled garlic clove, pine nuts and olive oil in a blender. Process, in short bursts, until smooth.
3. Add 1 tablespoonful of hot water and the cheese (grated) and blend again until creamy. This is now a pesto sauce.
4. Boil the pasta in slightly salted water until soft.
5. Drain the pasta and pan fry them in a little butter for 1 minute.
6. Add in a little of the pesto sauce and stir well before serving.

TIP

The pesto sauce will keep in a jar for quite a while because of the olive oil. Keep it in the fridge to use with vegetables such as potatoes and mushrooms. Finally, remember to use the pesto sauce sparingly; save it for your own meals.

RATATOUILLE (WITH BROWN RICE)

Age	1 year upwards
Preparation time	15 minutes
Cooking time	10 minutes
Serves	3

This delicious vegetarian recipe
has wonderful flavours and, served with a little brown rice, makes a substantial
meal for babies and young children. The dominant taste is tomato and peppers, so don't
go to town on this one unless you are sure your young diners like the taste.

INGREDIENTS

1 medium-sized onion
1 medium-sized pepper
1 clove garlic
½ lb (225g) of courgettes
½ lb (225g) of aubergines
½ lb (225g) of tomatoes
fresh parsley, chives and thyme
(chopped)
vegetable oil

METHOD

1. Peel and chop the onion, deseed and slice the pepper and crush the garlic.
2. Heat a little vegetable oil in a large saucepan and fry the onions, garlic and peppers for about 5 minutes.
3. Slice the courgettes thinly and dice the aubergines into small ¼ inch cubes before adding them. Then skin and chop the tomatoes and add these to the mixture. Stir gently and cook uncovered for about 5 minutes.
4. Sprinkle generously with the mixed, finely chopped herbs.
5. Serve with brown rice (well cooked).

TIP

Brown rice is perhaps the best accompaniment, but you can use potatoes or pasta, or just plain boiled white rice.

Spanish Omelette

Age	12 months upwards
Preparation time	15 minutes
Cooking time	25 minutes
Serves	3

Years ago (when I was a boy!),
omelette used to be a staple diet with lots of extras and flavourings. Nowadays,
we hardly seem to cook them. Let's bring omelettes back again – I like them! The key
item, of course, is the 'filling'. I have listed a handful of variations in
addition to the cheese suggestion. You will no doubt try out your own ideas though.

INGREDIENTS

2 potatoes
olive oil
1 onion
3 tablespoons green and red pepper
2 oz (50g) button mushrooms
1 tablespoon fresh parsley
  (chopped)
1 tablespoon fresh Parmesan cheese
1 tablespoon Gruyére cheese
salt and pepper
4 eggs

METHOD

1. Peel and dice the potato and fry in a little oil until golden brown. Drain off the liquid then set the potatoes aside.
2. Peel and finely chop the onion and fry with a little oil. After a few minutes add the chopped peppers.
3. When the onions have turned golden brown, add the washed and sliced mushroom and chopped parsley and cook over a medium heat for about another 3 minutes, stirring continuously.
4. Combine the onion mixture with the potatoes and the grated Parmesan in a large mixing bowl, and add any variation ingredients (in this case the Gruyére cheese). Season to taste.
5. Beat the eggs and pour them over the vegetable mixture.

SUGGESTED VARIATIONS

1 large tomato
1 tablespoon tomato ketchup
or
2 oz (50g) peas
1 tablespoon chives
or
2 oz (50g) tuna
9 oz (250g) chopped tomato
or
4 oz (100g) cooked ham or bacon
  (cubed)

6. Heat 2 tablespoonfuls of oil in a frying pan and tip the pan to coat halfway up the sides.
7. Fry the whole mixture for about 8–10 minutes until the omelette is lightly browned underneath. Finally, place under a hot grill for about 3 minutes until the surface is brown and crispy.
8. Cut into wedges. Serve hot or cold.

TIP
When cold, this dish can be a useful 'finger food' – a nutritious and healthy snack.

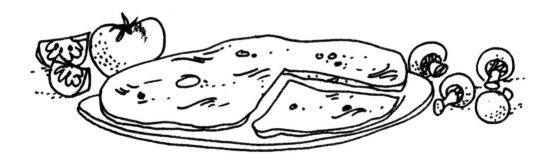

VEGETABLE RISSOLES

Age	1 year upwards
Preparation time	20 minutes
Cooking time	20 minutes
Serves	4

The word rissole usually denotes a small potato ball cooked until crispy.
However, you don't need to use potato to make rissoles, but if you like you can substitute
the cabbage with 6 oz (175g) of creamed potato.

INGREDIENTS

1 onion
2 oz (50g) young leeks
vegetable oil
6 oz (175g) cauliflower
6 oz (175g) cabbage
6 oz (175g) courgettes
salt and pepper
8 oz (225g) mushrooms
lemon juice
2 oz (50g) plain flour
2 teaspoons Marmite
2 fl oz (50ml) of hot water
*6 slices wholemeal or granary
    breadcrumbs*
1 egg

METHOD

1. Peel and finely chop the onion and leek. Fry in a little oil until transparent.
2. Meanwhile break the cauliflower up into florets, shred the cabbage and slice the courgette. Boil until tender with a little salt to taste.
3. When the onions are cooked, stir in the chopped mushrooms and fry for a further 3 minutes. Add the lemon juice.
4. Roughly chop the cooked cauliflower, cabbage and courgettes and add to the mushrooms and onions.
5. Stir in the flour and mix well. Mix in the Marmite, melted in the hot water, and stir in a few of the breadcrumbs to thicken the mixture; make this into small rissoles.
6. Dip the rissoles into the beaten egg, then some extra flour, and, finally, into the breadcrumbs. Chill for 30 minutes to firm up before cooking.
7. Fry in hot oil until golden and crisp on both sides.

TIP

Remember to let the mixture cool down before attempting to make into rissoles.

BAKED BEAN BURGER

Age	3 months upwards
Preparation time	10 minutes
Cooking time	5 minutes
Serves	2

This particular recipe has a special place
in my memory because it was the first I ever presented on television.
It was prepared live, with children in attendance. The cooking went very well, but the
children wouldn't eat it . . . cut to camera 2. Since that time I have adapted
it slightly and made it a little bit more adventurous, and now I never get rejections!

INGREDIENTS

2 dessertspoons of baked beans
2 dessertspoons of grated cheese
1 egg yolk
4 dessertspoons of white
*   breadcrumbs*
2 dessertspoons of mashed and
*   creamed potatoes*
chopped chives
fresh parsley (chopped)
milk
1 dessertspoon of vegetable oil

METHOD

1. Mash the baked beans (see page 120) with the cheese, potato, egg yolk, herbs and 1 dessertspoon of the breadcrumbs.
2. Mould into small burgers, about 2 inches across, and dip into a saucer of milk, and then the remaining breadcrumbs.
3. Heat a little vegetable oil in a thick-bottomed frying pan. Fry the burgers for about 1 minute each side.
4. Serve warm with a little tomato sauce (see page 72).

TIP

This recipe, more than anything, introduces the idea of a homemade burger. Once you have found success with them, try all sorts of recipes and combinations. Vegetables, pulses, herbs are all good, and you can even use fish for non vegetarians.

BAKED BEAN PIE

Age	6 months upwards
Preparation time	10 minutes
Cooking time	60 minutes
Serves	4

INGREDIENTS

14 oz (375g) can baked beans
12 oz (325g) fresh spinach
2 oz (50g) unsalted butter
1 dessertspoon plain flour
4 fl oz (100ml) milk
1 oz (25g) fresh Parmesan cheese
    (grated)
2 large potatoes
2 fl oz (50ml) milk

METHOD

1. For the topping, peel and chop the potatoes and boil for about 20 minutes until soft. Drain off the water.
2. For the sauce, wash and chop the spinach and simmer with a little water over a low heat until soft. Drain well.
3. Combine half the butter, flour and milk to make a thick white sauce.
4. Take the saucepan off the heat and stir in the grated Parmesan cheese. Mix the cheese sauce with the cooked spinach. Mash the cooked potatoes together with the milk and nearly all the remaining butter.
5. Place the spinach sauce in a large ovenproof dish. Cover with the baked beans and spread the mashed potato over the top.
6. Bake in a medium preheated oven (B) for 10–15 minutes, then dab on small amounts of reserved butter onto the potato to form a crispy topping.
7. Serve luke warm.

TIP

This delicious recipe gets a bit hot! Leave it to stand a short while before serving.

Fricassée of Eggs with Tarragon

Age	3 months upwards
Preparation time	35 minutes
Cooking time	15 minutes
Serves	4

In this recipe I use eggs as an alternative to fish or meat simply because I feel eggs are not used enough in their cooked form. If you prefer, you can, of course, reduce the amount of eggs and add fish or chicken.

INGREDIENTS

7 fl oz (200ml) milk
½ onion
½ carrot
bayleaf
1 oz (25g) unsalted butter
2 level tablespoons flour
5 fl oz (150ml) soured cream
2 teaspoons fresh tarragon
salt and freshly ground pepper
6 eggs
2 oz (50g) packet frozen puff pastry

METHOD

1. The first job is to hard boil the eggs (7 minutes). Leave them to cool in cold water and then slice, reserving the yolk from one.
2. Chop the ½ onion and place in a saucepan with the milk, carrot and bayleaf. Bring to the boil and leave to infuse for 10 minutes, then strain.
3. Melt the butter and slowly stir in the flour. Remove from the heat and gradually stir in the milk, soured cream, bayleaf and seasoning.
4. Return to the heat and bring to boil, stirring all the time until the sauce thickens. Simmer for about 5 minutes.
5. Add the egg slices to the sauce and simmer.
6. Snip the tarragon and push the reserved hard boiled egg yolk through a sieve. Use these to garnish.
7. For pastry triangles, make sure the pastry is well thawed. Roll it out into an oblong; divide into two, lengthwise, and cut each strip into about 10 triangles. Bake in a hot preheated oven (C) for 12–15 minutes until golden brown.
8. Serve the egg fricassée in the warm pastry triangles.

CHEESE AND HAZELNUT HOT POT

Age	3 years upwards
Preparation time	20 minutes
Cooking time	25 minutes
Serves	4

INGREDIENTS

8 oz (225g) flat noodles
1 medium onion
1 oz (25g) unsalted butter
2 level tablespoons tomato purée
2 oz (50g) hazelnuts
8 oz (225g) cottage cheese
salt and freshly ground pepper
2 oz (50g) Lancashire cheese
1 tomato (chopped)
fresh parsley

THE SAUCE

1 oz (25g) unsalted butter
1 oz (25g) flour
1/2 pint (300ml) of milk
salt and freshly ground pepper

METHOD

1. For the sauce, melt the butter in a saucepan and slowly add the flour. Cook over a low heat for 2 minutes. Remove from the heat and carefully add the milk, stirring and blending all the time.
2. Return to the heat, bring to the boil and cook until thickened. Season with salt and pepper.
3. Cook the noodles in a saucepan of boiling water with the salt added until tender. Drain well.
4. Chop the onion and fry gently in butter until golden. Stir the noodles, onion and tomato into the sauce.
5. Add the tomato purée, finely chopped hazelnuts and cottage cheese. Mix thoroughly. Season to taste.
6. Transfer to a buttered ovenproof dish and crumble the cheese over the top. Bake in a preheated medium oven (B) for 25 minutes, until golden brown.
7. Sprinkle with parsley and chives and serve.

TIP

This dish is delicious served hot with green vegetables.

BABY RICE AND VEGETABLES

Age	6 months upwards
Preparation time	10 minutes
Cooking time	35 minutes
Serves	3

This is similar to a purée
and is an ideal way of introducing some vegetables into a child's diet
at an early stage.

INGREDIENTS

¹/₄ small onion
2 courgettes
2 oz (50g) broccoli
2 medium carrots
1 oz (25g) green cabbage
vegetable stock
3 tablespoons baby rice

METHOD

1. Peel and finely chop the onion and carrots. Trim the courgettes, shred the cabbage and cut the broccoli into florets.
2. Place all of the vegetables in a saucepan and pour in the vegetable stock (see page 58).
3. Bring to the boil and simmer for 15 minutes or until the vegetables are tender.
4. Add the baby rice and stir over a gentle heat for 2 minutes.
5. Purée the mixture in a blender until the desired smooth consistency is attained.

TIP

Baby rice is good to help thicken purées and can be used in most of the purée recipes.

8
SWEET DREAMS

INTRODUCTION

T he 'pudding' is the most indulgent and frivolous end to a meal. But for children it should be a treat and therefore only be given to them (in my opinion) if they have eaten the previous courses. I know sometimes it's impossible, but if you give them the pudding when they have refused the main meal, you run the risk of them always refusing the main meal. So if they've been good, treat them and at the same time treat yourself.

Gone are the days of a proper pudding at the end of each meal. Nowadays, a yoghurt or a piece of fruit suffice unless it's a special occasion, party or holiday of some kind. If you want to create good fun and 'cheer' there is nothing nicer than a delicious homecooked pud. Sweet dreams!

PINEAPPLE PRIZES

Age	1 year upwards
Preparation time	15 minutes
Cooking time	25 minutes
Serves	4

Cooking fresh pineapple brings out a wonderful flavour.
Here the pineapple is cut into pieces and wrapped with a delicious black
cherry yoghurt. Save some for your child!

INGREDIENTS

1 medium pineapple
juice of 1 lemon
¼ (150ml) pint water
4 oz (100g) demerara sugar
3 oz (75g) fresh black cherries
*¼ pint (150ml) of black cherry
   yoghurt*

METHOD

1. Cut the pineapple across in rings and then cut the peel off.
2. Cut the rings into small pieces and discard the core.
3. Put the pineapple pieces in a saucepan and add the lemon juice to the water and boil for 15–20 minutes.
4. Add demerara sugar and boil again to dissolve it, until the sauce has become a syrup.
5. Allow to cool and when cold, spoon over the yoghurt and chill.
6. Serve and garnish with stoned cherries or even black seedless grapes.

TIP

You can use other fruits in the same way such as apples, pears and any hard fruits. You can also make this pudding look very attractive by placing it on a large platter or plate with the top of the pineapple, complete with leaves. Ideal for parties!

COCONUT ICE-CREAM WITH MANGO COULIS

Age	6 months upwards
Preparation time	15 minutes
Cooking time	10 minutes
Serves	6

This delicious recipe originates from Indonesia.
The pearly white ice-cream sits in the centre of a brilliant orange coulis
(purée) so it looks really attractive. They might just stick their hands in it but let them learn
to appreciate colours and interesting flavours like these!

INGREDIENTS

6 oz (175g) dessicated coconut
1 pint (575ml) double cream
¾ pint (450ml) milk
½ oz (15g) gelatine
3 tablespoons water
4 oz (100g) castor sugar
1 teaspoon salt
oil, for greasing

INGREDIENTS FOR THE COULIS

1 ripe mango
1 tablespoon castor sugar
juice of 1 lemon
juice of 1 orange

METHOD

1. Put the coconut into a saucepan and add ¼ pint (150ml) of the cream and all of the milk. Bring slowly to the boil.
2. Cover the pan, turn off the heat, and leave to infuse for 10 minutes.
3. Dissolve the gelatine in the water in a small saucepan over a low heat.
4. Add to the coconut and cream mixture with the castor sugar and salt.
5. Liquidize the mixture for approximately 1 minute.
6. Sieve the mixture into a mixing bowl pressing the coconut debris thoroughly with a wooden spoon.
7. Leave the bowl in a cool place until cold and thick.
8. In another bowl, whisk the remaining ¾ pint (450ml) of cream until thick and then thoroughly fold in to the coconut mixture.
9. Lightly oil a pudding basin and pour in the ice-cream mixture. Freeze for at least 5 hours.

10. Meanwhile, cut the mango in half and scrape out all of the flesh with a metal spoon into a liquidizer. Add the castor sugar and the strained lemon and orange juice. Blend well.

11. About two hours before eating, dip the pudding basin in a sink of very hot water for about a minute, then turn out the ice-cream onto the centre of a large, flat serving plate.

12. Spoon the mango purée around the ice-cream and put back in the fridge for the next 2 hours before eating.

TIP

This recipe also works well with various other fruit coulis, like raspberry, strawberry etc. (See page 163 for coulis recipe.)

SIMPLE CHOCOLATE MOUSSE

Age	2 years upwards
Preparation time	15 minutes
Cooking time	10 minutes
Serves	4

This recipe is so simple – your child
could prepare it for you! The secret of a good chocolate mousse is the
quality of the chocolate. Don't be mean when buying for this, if you use good chocolate
the whole family will enjoy this dish.

INGREDIENTS

3 eggs
3 oz (75g) of good plain chocolate

METHOD

1. Break the chocolate into pieces and place in a small basin.
2. Stand the basin over a pot of boiling water and melt. Make sure that the basin does not actually touch the water.
3. Separate the eggs, put whites in a mixing bowl and whisk until they peak.
4. Remove melted chocolate, stir in yolks and then gradually fold in whites gently – do not mix too much.
5. Pour into small dishes and allow to set.

TIP

You can add a touch of brandy or Cointreau to half of the mix and eat it yourself – but remember which half is which!

Banana Clouds

Age	1 year upwards
Preparation time	15 minutes
Cooking time	none
Serves	4

Yet another very simple and quick recipe,
but really tasty. I always have to taste it as I'm preparing it and eventually
end up with only a dessertspoonful for the children!

INGREDIENTS

3 bananas
2 egg whites
1 oz (25g) castor sugar
juice from ½ a lemon

METHOD

1. Peel the bananas and mash with a fork, and add the lemon juice.
2. Put egg whites in a basin and whisk until it peaks.
3. Add the banana and sugar and continue to whisk until quite stiff.
4. Pour into serving dishes.

TIP

After the many scares about raw eggs, I tend to whisk the whites over a pan of boiling water to actually cook them (Sabayon) before adding to the banana mix. It makes me feel better anyway!

STEVEN'S SPECIAL CHOCOLATE TART

Age	1 year upwards
Preparation time	25 minutes
Cooking time	30 minutes
Serves	4

If you feel in a baking mood
this recipe for chocolate tart is truly mind-blowing! The combination
of orange with butter chocolate is delightful. Its delicate chocolate pastry and light, frothy
orange filling looks and tastes wonderful.

INGREDIENTS
FOR THE PASTRY

6 oz (175g) self-raising flour
1 tablespoon of cocoa powder
3 oz (75g) icing sugar
4 oz (100g) unsalted butter
1 tablespoon water

FOR THE FILLING

3 eggs (separated)
2 oz (50g) castor sugar
juice of 2 oranges
4 tablespoons double cream
1 oz (25g) cornflour
finely grated zest of 1 orange

FOR THE
CHOCOLATE ICING

6 oz (175g) plain chocolate
4 teaspoons castor sugar

METHOD TO MAKE PASTRY

1. Sift flour, cocoa powder and icing sugar into a bowl.
2. Melt butter gently with water and pour into the flour mixture. Mix thoroughly with a spoon to form a dough.
3. Press the warm dough evenly and neatly into an aluminium loose-based flan tin with fluted sides.
4. Refrigerate for at least 30 minutes. Remember to preheat the oven to B.

METHOD TO MAKE FILLING

1. Put the yolks in a bowl, add the sugar and whisk until pale and thick.
2. Gradually whisk in the orange juice, followed by the cream.
3. Then whisk in the cornflour (mixed with a little cream) and stir in the grated zest of orange.
4. In a separate bowl, whisk the egg whites until they peak and fold gently into the orange mix.

5. Pour into the chilled pastry case and bake in the centre of the oven for 20–25 minutes.

METHOD TO MAKE CHOCOLATE ICING

1. Melt the chocolate with the sugar and 1½ table-spoons of cold water over a low heat and stir until smooth.
2. Remove from heat and stir in another 2 teaspoons of cold water.
3. Pour mix over the tart and spread with a palette knife.
4. Leave to cool and dust a little icing sugar over the top. Serve cold, but not from the fridge.

TIP

If chocolate is put into the fridge it sweats and will become soggy and watery. Ideally, keep the tart in a pantry – if anyone has one of those these days!

CARROT CAKE

Age	1 year upwards
Preparation time	20 minutes
Cooking time	50 minutes
Serves	12

All the family seem to like this one
and it tastes a lot nicer than it sounds – promise!

INGREDIENTS

12 oz (325g) wholemeal
    self-raising flour
1 teaspoon bicarbonate of soda
1 teaspoon mixed spice
8 oz (225g) granulated sugar
6 fl oz (175ml) vegetable oil
3 eggs (beaten)
4 oz (100g) carrot
6 oz (175g) fresh pineapple
2 oz (50g) walnuts

METHOD

1. The first step is to grease two 1 lb loaf tins, lining the base and both ends of each tin with a strip of greased greaseproof paper – long enough to overhang the ends by about 1 inch on each side.
2. Place the flour in a bowl and mix well with the bicarbonate of soda, spice and sugar.
3. Make a well in the centre of the mixture, pour in the oil and beaten eggs, and mix thoroughly to form a smooth mixture.
4. Grate the carrot, chop the walnuts and purée the pineapple.
5. Fold the carrot, pineapple and chopped walnuts into the mixture, trying to trap as much air as possible. Spoon the batter into the tins and smooth the surface.
6. Bake in a preheated moderate oven (B) for 50 minutes. Turn the cake out onto a wire rack and leave to cool.

TIP

If you would like it to be a more savoury, less sweet cake, double the amount of grated carrot and reduce the pineapple by half.

TRADITIONAL FRUIT CAKE (FOR BIRTHDAYS, ETC.)

Age	1 year upwards
Preparation time	2 hours 30 minutes
Cooking time	3 hours 30 minutes
Serves	20

There is very little more
that can be said about this traditional and wonderful recipe. It's in this
book because children ought to acquire a taste for it early in life.

INGREDIENTS

12 oz (325g) currants
12 oz (325g) sultanas
12 oz (325g) raisins
6 fl oz (175ml) orange juice
8 oz (225g) margarine or butter
5 oz (140g) brown sugar
4 eggs
4 oz (100g) walnuts
4 oz (100g) glacé cherries
8 oz (225g) plain flour
1 teaspoon baking soda
1/2 teaspoon salt
2 teaspoons powdered cinnamon
1 teaspoon ground ginger
1 teaspoon allspice

METHOD

1. Sprinkle the dried fruit with the orange juice and leave for about 2 hours.
2. Cream the margarine together with the sugar then beat in the eggs one at a time. Add the fruits and their liquid, the chopped walnuts and cherries.
3. Mix together all the remaining dry ingredients and fold these into the cake mix.
4. Line the bottom of a 10 inch, round cake tin with greased greaseproof paper and pour in the cake mix.
5. Bake in a slow preheated oven (A) for 3½ hours. Leave to cool, then store in an airtight container.

TIP

A good, general recipe for birthday cake bases or Christmas and Easter cakes. Leave out the walnuts if you know really young children will be eating the fruit cake.

REAL BLANCMANGE

Age	3 months upwards
Preparation time	15 minutes
Cooking time	10 minutes
Serves	4

One of my old favourites.
I remember my mum making this superb vanilla blancmange. I have
added some variations which you may not have tried yourself.

INGREDIENTS

4 level tablespoons cornflour
1 pint (575ml) milk
strip of lemon rind
3 level teaspoons castor sugar
1 vanilla pod split in half

METHOD

1. Use a small amount of milk from the pint and blend together with the cornflour to form a smooth paste.
2. Add the strip of lemon rind and the vanilla pod to the remaining milk and boil. Strain into the blended cornflour mixture stirring well.
3. Return the mixture to the pan and bring to the boil, stirring all the time, until it thickens. Cook for a further 3 minutes and add sugar to taste.
4. Pour the liquid into a suitably sized jelly mould and leave for several hours until set.
5. Serve turned out onto a dish decorated with colourful fresh fruit.

VARIATIONS

1. Instead of adding lemon, use either 2 oz (50g) of melted chocolate to the cooked mixture, or a fruit purée of your choice.
2. Instead of lemon rind, add either 2 tablespoonfuls of coffee essence or 1 level teaspoonful of grated orange rind.
3. Instead of castor sugar, use a little honey.

TIP

Do not use vanilla essence which is loaded with artificial flavourings and additives. The natural pods are much better.

HONEY FOOL

Age   1 year upwards
Preparation time soaking overnight plus 15 minutes
Cooking time   none
Serves   6

INGREDIENTS

12 oz (325g) dried fruit – apricots,
 peaches, pears, prunes, apples
2 ripe bananas
lemon juice
1 tablespoon clear honey
¼ pint (150ml) fresh double cream

METHOD

1. The dried fruit needs to be soaked overnight in cold water and drained well before use.
2. Peel and slice the bananas. A few slices should be dipped in lemon juice and reserved for decoration.
3. The remaining banana, dried fruit and honey should be put into a blender and processed until smooth.
4. Whip the fresh cream until stiff but still relatively soft, and fold into the fruit mixture.
5. Spoon into individual dishes and chill.
6. Decorate with slices of banana.

TIP

This recipe is just as nice with fresh fruits, but dried fruits are convenient and very good to use in recipes of this kind.

STRAWBERRY SYLLABUB

Age	6 months upwards
Preparation time	20 minutes
Cooking time	none
Serves	4–6

INGREDIENTS

8 oz (225g) strawberries
1 egg white
3 oz (75g) icing sugar
¼ pint (150ml) fresh double cream

METHOD

1. Remove stalks from the strawberries, but do not wash them. Wipe if really necessary but the berries need to remain dry.
2. Place in a bowl and mash with a stainless potato masher.
3. Add the icing sugar and egg white and whisk until thick and frothy.
4. Separately whip the fresh cream until stiff, then gently fold into the strawberry mixture.
5. Pour the mixture into tall glasses, filling to the top. Chill for approximately 6 hours before serving.
7. Decorate with fresh whipped cream, and halved strawberries.

COTTAGE CHEESE AND FRUIT MOUSSE

Age	1 year upwards
Preparation time	30 minutes
Cooking time	none
Serves	10

INGREDIENTS

4 oz (100g) castor sugar
4 oz (100g) blackcurrants
4 oz (100g) red currants
1/4 pint (150ml) of water
7 level teaspoons gelatine
4 oz (100g) raspberries
1 orange
1 lemon
1/4 pint (150ml) soured cream
12 oz (325g) cottage cheese
2 eggs
1/4 pint (150ml) fresh double cream

METHOD

1. Top and tail the blackcurrants and redcurrants and hull the raspberries.
2. Dissolve 1 oz (25g) sugar in 1/4 pint (150ml) of water. Add the prepared currants and simmer slowly until fruit is tender, but not mushy.
3. In a cup or small bowl, sprinkle 2 level teaspoonfuls of gelatine over 2 tablespoonfuls of water and leave for a few minutes. Remove the fruit from the heat and add the gelatine mixture, stirring until dissolved.
4. Cool the fruit mixture and add the raspberries. When it begins to set, pour into a ring mould and chill.
5. Remove the juice and grate the rind from the orange and lemon and mix with the remaining castor sugar, soured cream, cottage cheese and egg yolks. Blend until smooth.
6. Dissolve the remaining gelatine in 3 tablespoonfuls of water in a small bowl over a pan of hot water. Add to cheese mixture and mix well. When this is done, turn out into a serving bowl.
7. Whip the fresh cream until stiff but still soft. Fold into the cheese mixture.
8. Whisk the egg whites until stiff, then whisk in the remaining sugar. Fold into the cheese mixture and then pour into a mould. Chill thoroughly until set and turn out from mould to serve.

TIP

If currants and raspberries are out of season, use dried fruits in similar quantities.

FRESH PINEAPPLE CHEESECAKE

Age	1 year upwards
Preparation time	30 minutes
Cooking time	none
Serves	10

My two love this!
The first time I ever heard Stefanie (now 19 months)
say 'more' was for this recipe!

INGREDIENTS

3 oz (75g) unsalted butter
6 oz (175g) plain chocolate
   wholewheat biscuits
8 oz (225g) cottage cheese
4 oz (100g) full-fat soft cheese
1 large lemon
1/4 pint (150ml) natural yoghurt
3 eggs
2 oz (50g) castor sugar
3 level teaspoons gelatine
4 oz (100g) fresh pineapple
4 level tablespoons apricot jam

METHOD

1. Roughly crush the biscuits. Melt the butter in a pan and add the biscuit mixture combining the two.
2. Press the mixture into a 9 inch spring-release cake tin, then refrigerate for several hours.
3. Sieve the cottage cheese and then blend together with the full-fat soft cheese, the lemon rind, 3 table-spoonfuls of lemon juice and the yoghurt. This should be a smooth mixture.
4. Whisk together the egg yolks and sugar until thick.
5. Soak the gelatine in 3 tablespoons of water in a small bowl. Dissolve by standing the bowl in a pan of simmering water. This should then be whisked into the egg yolks along with the cheese mixture.
6. Slice approximately three-quarters of the pineapple, reserving the juice.

7. Whisk the egg whites until stiff and fold into the setting cheese mixture together with the chopped pineapple.

8. Pour into the crust and refrigerate until set.

9. Carefully remove the sides of the cake tin then, using a fish slice, lift and slide the cheesecake off the base onto a serving plate.

10. The remaining pineapple is used to decorate the top of the cheesecake. Sieve the jam and boil down a thick glaze, cool and then spoon over the pineapple.

TIP
Although fresh pineapple is best, tinned pineapple is a suitable alternative.

BAKED CUSTARD WITH NUTMEG

Age	3 months upwards
Preparation time	15 minutes
Cooking time	45 minutes
Serves	4

INGREDIENTS

1 pint (575ml) milk
3 eggs
2 level tablespoons castor sugar

METHOD

1. Warm the milk in a saucepan but do not bring to the boil.
2. Whisk together the eggs and sugar. Pour into the hot milk, stirring continuously.
3. Strain the mixture into a buttered ovenproof dish.
4. Bake in a medium oven (B) for about 45 minutes, until the mixture is set and firm to the touch.

TIP

This simple but delicious dish should be served cold and is best accompanied with slices of fresh fruit, or fruit purée coulis sauce (see page 163).

YOGHURT SCONES

Age	18 months upwards
Preparation time	15 minutes
Cooking time	40 minutes
Serves	8

These are an interesting derivative
of the more usual scone. They are full of flavour and very light and fluffy.

INGREDIENTS

½ teaspoon baking powder
¼ teaspoon bicarbonate of soda
1 lb (450g) flour
1 teaspoon salt
½ tablespoon sugar
10 oz (275g) natural yoghurt
¼ pint (150ml) water

METHOD

1. Measure out the dry ingredients and then sift together into a bowl.
2. Stir in the natural yoghurt and about ¼ pint (150ml) water until the mixture forms a smooth dough.
3. Knead the dough lightly and shape into one large 6 inch round or small individual scones.
4. Place on a greased baking sheet and bake in a medium preheated oven (B) for about 40 minutes until the base sounds hollow when tapped.

TIP

If you make individual scones cook them for less time, approximately 30 minutes. By placing a tray of boiling water at the bottom of the oven you will increase the light consistency of your scones by creating a steamy atmosphere.

PEACH SCONE

Age	18 months upwards
Preparation time	15 minutes
Cooking time	25 minutes
Serves	4

INGREDIENTS

4 oz (100g) self-raising flour
½ level teaspoon mixed spice
1 oz (25g) unsalted butter
2 level teaspoons castor sugar
4 tablespoons milk
4 oz (100g) fresh peaches
¼ pint (150ml) soured cream
1 level tablespoon demerara sugar

METHOD

1. Sift together the flour and spice. Use your fingertips to rub in the butter until the mixture resembles fine breadcrumbs.
2. Stir in the sugar and mix to a soft dough with the milk.
3. Pat out on a buttered baking tray to a 7 inch round; crimp the edges.
4. Decorate the top with slices of peach to form a spiral. Spread the soured cream over the fruit and sprinkle with demerara sugar.
5. Bake in a high preheated oven (C) for about 25 minutes.

SYRUP SCONES

Age	18 months upwards
Preparation time	20 minutes
Cooking time	15 minutes
Makes 20 scones	

INGREDIENTS

12 oz (325g) self-raising flour
1½ teaspoons baking powder
½ teaspoon ground ginger
3 oz (75g) unsalted butter
2 oz (50g) porridge oats
4 tablespoons golden syrup
7 fl oz (200ml) milk

METHOD

1. Sift together the flour, baking powder and ground ginger. Using fingertips, rub in the butter until the mixture resembles fine breadcrumbs.
2. Stir in the oats.
3. Slowly warm the syrup and add to the milk, which needs to be at room temperature.
4. Using the milk and syrup, mix the dry ingredients to a soft dough. It may be necessary to add more milk if the mixture becomes dry.
5. With a floured rolling pin, roll the dough out to ½ inch thick and divide into 3 inch rounds. Repeat until the dough is used up.
6. Place the scones on buttered preheated baking trays. Brush with milk and bake in a high oven (C) for 10–12 minutes.

TIP

These scones should be served immediately, while still relatively hot.

UPSIDE-DOWN CURRANT BUNS

Age	3 years upwards
Preparation time	10 minutes
Cooking time	30 minutes
Serves	15

INGREDIENTS

2 level tablespoons currants
2 level tablespoons almonds
5 oz (140g) unsalted butter
5 oz (140g) castor sugar
2 eggs
1 lemon
4 oz (100g) flour

METHOD

1. Chop the almonds finely, divide these and the currants between 15 buttered bun moulds.
2. Place the butter and sugar in a bowl and whisk together until fluffy.
3. Grate the lemon rind and beat with the eggs into the mixture.
4. Sift over the flour and fold in.
5. Divide the mixture evenly between the tins and level off with a knife.
6. Bake in a preheated oven (B) for 25–30 minutes.
7. Once cooked, gently ease out of the tins and leave to cool on a wire rack.

TIP

These make a good treat to liven up your children's packed lunches.

DATE AND HONEY BARS

Age	18 months upwards
Preparation time	20 minutes
Cooking time	25 minutes
Serves	18

INGREDIENTS

6 oz (175g) dates
3 level tablespoons thick honey
2 tablespoons lemon juice
8 tablespoons water
2 level teaspoons plain flour
4 oz (100g) self-raising flour
4 oz (100g) demerara sugar
5 oz (140g) rolled oats
6 oz (175g) unsalted butter

METHOD

1. Butter a 7 inch square tin which is 1 inch deep.
2. Stone and chop the dates and place in a saucepan together with the honey, strained lemon juice, plain flour and 8 tablespoons water.
3. Stirring all the time, bring the mixture slowly to the boil. Cook gently for 3–4 minutes. Allow to cool.
4. Melt the butter and mix in the self-raising flour, sugar and oats. Spread half of this crumbly mixture over the base of the tin, pressing down well.
5. Add the date mixture on top, spreading evenly. Spread the remaining half of the crumbly mixture over this, pressing evenly all over the surface.
6. Bake in a medium oven (B) for about 25 minutes, until golden in colour. Remove from the oven and leave to cool in the tin for at least 30 minutes.
7. When well cooled, cut into bars and ease out of the tin.

TIP

These bars need to be stored in an airtight container and will last for a few days – handy for snacks and packed lunches.

PEANUT BUTTER COOKIES

Age   2 years upwards
Preparation time   15 minutes
Cooking time   10–12 minutes
Makes 25 cookies

INGREDIENTS

6 oz (175g) unsalted butter
2 oz (50g) smooth peanut butter
4 oz (100g) soft brown sugar
1 egg
5 oz (140g) flour
salt

METHOD

1. Blend together the butter, peanut butter, sugar and egg.
2. Add the flour and a little salt and mix into a dough.
3. Divide and roll the dough into 25 balls. Place these on a buttered baking tray and flatten with a fork.
4. Bake in a medium oven (B) for 10–12 minutes, until golden.

TIP

The cookies should be left to cool thoroughly. Any not eaten should be stored in an airtight container.

BANANA CAKE

Age	1 year upwards
Preparation time	15 minutes
Cooking time	25–30 minutes
Servings	10

If you like my apple cake (see page 204), you'll also love this one!

INGREDIENTS

4 oz (100g) unsalted butter
4 tablespoons clear honey
3 ripe bananas
2 eggs
4 oz (100g) plain wholemeal flour
2 teaspoons baking powder
1 teaspoon lemon juice
2 oz (50g) curd cheese
2 tablespoons ground almonds

METHOD

1. Mash two bananas and blend together with the butter and honey. Add the eggs, flour and baking powder and beat together thoroughly until smooth.
2. Grease two 7 inch sandwich tins and pour in $\frac{1}{2}$ of the mixture in each.
3. Bake in a medium preheated oven (B) for 20–25 minutes, until the cakes are springy to the touch. Turn out and cool on a wire rack.
4. To make the filling, mash the remaining banana with a small amount of lemon juice and then blend the ingredients together to form a smooth mixture.
5. Spread evenly over one of the cakes and carefully place the other on top. This cake is best eaten within 48 hours.

BANANA BROWNIES

Age	1 year upwards
Preparation time	15 minutes
Cooking time	25–35 minutes
Makes 16 brownies	

I have got a soft spot for these – hence,
they are always to be found lurking somewhere in my fridge!

INGREDIENTS

3 oz (75g) unsweetened carob or
    plain chocolate
4 tablespoons corn oil
4 tablespoons clear honey
4 oz (100g) self-raising wholemeal
    flour
2 tablespoons cold water
1 banana
2 eggs

METHOD

1. Break the carob or chocolate into pieces and place in a small pan together with the oil and honey. Heat gently until melted.
2. Sieve the flour into a mixing bowl and make a well in the centre. Beat in the carob/chocolate mixture with the water.
3. Mash the banana and beat this in together with the eggs. The mixture should be beaten well, until smooth.
4. Grease and line a 7 inch square, shallow cake tin and pour the mixture in. Bake in a medium preheated oven (B) for 25–30 minutes, until just beginning to shrink from the sides of the tin.
5. When cooked, remove from the tin and cool on a wire rack. Cut into small pieces to serve.

TIP

Serve warm with vanilla ice-cream! Yum.

GINGERBREAD MEN

Age	1 year upwards
Preparation time	20 minutes
Cooking time	10–15 minutes
Serves 10	

Have a glance at the recipe for 'space people'
see page 182 – the basic constituent is gingerbread too.

INGREDIENTS

4 oz (100g) plain wholemeal flour
½ teaspoon bicarbonate of soda
½ teaspoon ground cinnamon
1 teaspoon ground ginger
1 oz (25g) unsalted butter
2 oz (50g) muscovado sugar
1 tablespoon clear honey
1 teaspoon orange juice
2 oz (50g) curd cheese
a little milk to mix

METHOD

1. Sift the flour, soda and spices together in a bowl.
2. Warm the butter, sugar and honey in a pan, being careful to keep stirring and watching until the butter is melted.
3. Cool this mixture, then pour onto the flour mix with the orange juice and combine to form a firm dough.
4. On a floured board, roll out the dough until approximately ¼ inch thick. Using a gingerbread man cutter – or your own design! – cut out about 10 men and place on greased baking sheets.
5. Bake in a medium preheated oven (B) for 10–15 minutes, until firm. Cool on a wire rack.
6. For a filling, blend the curd cheese with a little milk to give a smooth consistency. Spoon into a greaseproof paper piping bag fitted with a writing nozzle. Carefully pipe the eyes, nose, mouth and buttons on each man.

FRESH RASPBERRY JELLY

Age	1 year upwards
Preparation time	15 minutes
Cooking time	15 minutes
Serves	4–6

This is a very easy fruit jelly,
ideal for kids' parties or just to keep in the fridge as a treat.

INGREDIENTS

4 punnets of fresh rasberries
1¼ pints (710ml) of water
4 oz (100g) castor sugar
5 leaves of gelatine
1 teaspoon of lemon juice
fresh nutmeg (grated)
½ stick of cinnamon
the juice from 2 oranges

METHOD

1. Put half of the water and sugar in a pan and boil until sugar dissolves. Add the cinnamon, nutmeg and fresh orange juice.
2. Put leaf of gelatine in a little cold water in a cup and stand the cup in a bowl of hot water until the gelatine dissolves.
3. Put the raspberries into a saucepan of boiling water and stir in the lemon juice.
4. Simmer for a few minutes and take off heat. Strain through a nylon sieve.
5. Add the gelatine and stir well.
6. Pour into a jelly mould (or small dishes) and chill till firm.
7. Turn out and garnish with a little whipped cream or yoghurt.

TIP

You can, of course, use other fruits like peaches, strawberries, nectarines, pears or plums, etc.

YOGHURT FOOL

Age	1 year upwards
Preparation time	10 minutes
Cooking time	none
Serves	6

INGREDIENTS

1 fresh sponge cake approximately 6 × 6 inches (you can use a bought sponge for this if you want)

grated rind and the juice of 4 oranges

grated rind and the juice of 2 lemons

3 oz (25g) castor sugar

1 pint (575ml) of fruit yoghurt

METHOD

1. Mix the orange and lemon juice with the sugar until it dissolves. Line individual serving dishes (ramekins/ small dishes) with the sponge, up the sides as well.
2. Whisk the yoghurt slightly to ensure that it is nice and thick.
3. Pour the juice mix over the sponge while also using a spoon to ladle over the sides to ensure a good soaking.
4. Finally, pour the yoghurt into the dishes and set in the fridge for several hours until well chilled.

TIP

If you can get hold of tall, plastic, clear glasses, another adaptation of this is to put fresh fruit at the bottom. Pour on the juice mix and pipe on the yoghurt, whilst pressing down firmly, spiralling the yoghurt (clockwise) so that the juice spins up the side of the glasses and looks attractive. Another useful party pudding.

SUMMER PUDDING

Age	1 year upwards
Preparation time	10 minutes
Cooking time	10 minutes
Serves	4–6

This classic pud was originally devised
in the eighteenth century for those who could not digest rich desserts!
Good for all of the family.

INGREDIENTS

*1 lb (450g) of soft fresh fruits
(raspberries, blackberries,
loganberries, redcurrants,
blackcurrants, stoned cherries,
etc.)*
2 oz (50g) sugar
juice of ¼ lemon
4–5 thin slices of white bread
2 pints (1.1l) of water
½ stick of cinammon

METHOD

1. Bring the water and cinnamon to the boil, add the fresh fruits and lemon juice. Boil until fruit starts to break up and the juices run.
2. Remove crusts from the bread and use to line a deep pudding bowl, trim to fit.
3. Ladle in the fruit, soaking the bread at the same time, and cover with the remaining bread.
4. Put a saucer and a heavy weight over the top of the bowl and chill overnight.
5. Turn out onto a plate, decorate and serve.

TIP

This pud can be frozen after stage 4, but thaw overnight in your fridge.

FRUIT COULIS (PURÉES)

Coulis can be made from vegetables or fruits. It is a very useful finely puréed sauce and makes an excellent accompaniment to puddings (or in vegetable form, to main dishes). I usually have a selection of various coulis in the fridge kept in plastic airtight containers. They keep for up to about a week.

PASSION FRUIT COULIS

Age	1 year upwards
Preparation time	15 minutes
Cooking time	5 minutes
Serves	6

INGREDIENTS

12 passion fruits
1 large orange
2½ oz (65g) castor sugar
2 fl oz (50ml) water

METHOD

1. Halve the passion fruits, remove the seeds and pulp with a spoon. Keep in a bowl.
2. Halve the orange and squeeze all the juice onto the passion fruit.
3. Add the sugar and water and liquidize for 20 seconds.
4. Now boil the pulp in a small saucepan for 2 minutes.
5. Strain through a nylon sieve using a ladle or spoon to force it through.
6. Cool, cover with clingfilm and keep in the fridge.

TIP

Although there are many ways of making a coulis, this method can be perfected with most fruits. Generally, cooking the fruit for a couple of minutes enables you to extract more juice.

VANILLA CUSTARD

Age	1 year upwards
Preparation time	15 minutes
Cooking time	15 minutes
Serves	6

This is a recipe we use widely for puddings at the restaurant. This delicious, sweet, smooth custard sauce is a great accompaniment to all types of fresh fruits, cakes, ice-creams, etc. It can also be used as a base to make ice-cream.

INGREDIENTS

6 egg yolks
2½ oz (65g) castor sugar
2 split vanilla pods
18 fl oz (500ml) milk

METHOD

1. In a large bowl, cream together the egg yolks and sugar until a pale colour.
2. Put milk and vanilla pods in a heavy-bottomed saucepan and bring to the boil. Simmer for 5 minutes. Draw off heat and cool for 30 seconds.
3. Pour the milk onto the eggs and sugar, whisking continuously and return the sauce to the heavy-bottomed saucepan.
4. On a medium heat, stir the sauce until it thickens (keep stirring continuously until it coats the back of your spoon).
5. Strain the sauce through a nylon sieve, allow to cool and keep in the fridge.

TIP

You can experiment with variations of this sauce by adding lemon zest to the milk for a lemon custard, or orange zest and a touch of fresh orange juice.

9
PARTY TIME

INTRODUCTION

Parties are great fun! The only problem is that they really need a lot of organization, planning and time to create fun and tasty food that will be enjoyed by all, including Mum and Dad! So many people turn out 'junk' type food for parties – it worries me! Crisps in all different shapes, sausages on sticks, jelly and ice-cream and cheese sandwiches are boring and not particularly nutritious. Try some of these more 'creative' ideas – we have found them enormously successful with both parents and children. Most people have said they could never compete with our display and party food! That is actually not true, with a little help anyone can produce a party that will be remembered always, without costing a fortune! I hope this is of some help. Save me a piece of cake! (See also chapter 10 for further ideas.)

CHICKEN, ONION AND SWEETCORN POTATO CAKES

Age	1 year upwards
Preparation time	20 minutes
Cooking time	20 minutes
Serves	4

This is a good 'snacky' type of meal, ideal for children's parties and special occasions.

INGREDIENTS

7 fl oz (200ml) milk
2 eggs
4 oz (100g) flour
1 lb (450g) potatoes
8 oz (225g) onion
8 oz (225g) cooked chicken
7 oz (200g) can sweetcorn
unsalted butter
vegetable oil
salt

METHOD

1. Make a batter about 1 hour before cooking by whisking the milk and eggs together, beating in the flour and adding a pinch of salt. Do this until it is smooth – then keep cool until needed.
2. Peel the potatoes and onion. Coarsely grate the former and thinly slice the latter before blanching them together for about 2–3 minutes.
3. Drain the vegetables together and press down on them lightly – enough to squeeze out moisture but not too much to destroy the structure.
4. Cut the chicken very fine and stir small pieces into the batter. To this add the sweetcorn (drained), potato and onion. At this stage, also, add a little salt.
5. Heat the butter and oil together in equal proportions until the bottom of a pan is covered by about $1/4$ inch. Spoon heaped tablespoonfuls of the batter mix into this.
6. In cooking, keep the cakes pressed down into the oil, turning occasionally.
7. Drain well and keep the first cakes warm until all the mix is used. Serve warm.

TIP

Fish and sweetcorn work just as well together as chicken and sweetcorn, but use firm fish such as salmon, cod or monkfish.

BARBECUED SPICY CHICKEN DRUMSTICKS

Age	3 years upwards
Preparation time	30 minutes
Cooking time	20–30 minutes
Serves	4

A good summer-time recipe – again,
for all the family but remember to adjust the levels of spicing for younger
children.

INGREDIENTS

8 chicken drumsticks
1 medium onion
1 clove garlic
14 oz (375g) fresh tomatoes
1 tablespoon lemon juice
1 tablespoon soy sauce or
*   Worcestershire sauce*
2 teaspoons brown sugar
2 teaspoons oil

METHOD

1. Peel and finely chop the onion, chop the tomatoes and crush the garlic clove. Place in a mixing bowl with the lemon juice, Worcestershire sauce, brown sugar and oil.
2. Wipe the chicken thoroughly and coat with the sauce, leaving some for basting. Leave to marinate for 20 minutes or more (if baking in the oven remove the chicken skins before marinating – see below).
3. Barbecue the chicken, frequently basting it with the remaining sauce during the period of cooking. Alternatively, you can cook the chicken in the conventional way by baking it in a high preheated oven (C) for 30 minutes.
4. Check that the drumsticks are cooked by inserting a skewer into the flesh: the juices should be clear.

TIP

Remember to light your barbecue at least 30–40 minutes before you start to cook. The best barbecued food is cooked on white-hot coals without a flame. It is a good idea to remove the chicken bones before serving up this dish – young children over 3 should be okay.

COTTAGE CHEESE DIP

Age	6 months upwards
Preparation time	10 minutes
Cooking time	none
Serves	8

INGREDIENTS

1 pint (575ml) of cottage cheese
2 tablespoons cream cheese
Worcestershire sauce to taste
1 dessertspoon chopped spring
   onions or chives
freshly ground salt and pepper

METHOD

1. Finely chop the spring onions or chives and thoroughly mix with the other ingredients.
2. Serve with a selection of fresh, crunchy vegetables cut into sticks or strips of pitta bread to dip in.

TIP
Sultanas added to the dip can make a pleasant variation of taste.

CHEESE STRAWS WITH TOMATO

Age	2 years upwards
Preparation time	30 minutes
Cooking time	10 minutes
Makes about 65 straws	

Another good recipe suitable for snacks
or parties. Before cooking, you can mould them into number or letter
shapes for added visual interest.

INGREDIENTS

4 oz (100g) plain wholemeal flour
2 oz (50g) unsalted butter
3 oz (75g) Cheddar cheese
1 egg yolk
2–3 teaspoons cold water
2 tablespoons tomato purée

METHOD

1. Sift the flour into a bowl and, using your fingertips, rub in the butter until the mixture reaches a bread-crumb consistency.
2. Roughly grate the cheese and stir in.
3. Blend together the egg yolk, water and tomato purée, add to the flour mixture and mix to a firm dough.
4. Turn onto a lightly floured surface and knead lightly until smooth. Roll out thinly into a 9 inch square, then cut into 3 × ¼ inch strips.
5. Place on a baking sheet and bake in a high preheated oven (C) for 8–10 minutes, until golden. Cool on a wire rack.

TREASURE PURSES

Age   1 year upwards
Preparation time   15 minutes
Cooking time   25 minutes
Makes 30 'purses'

These make a delightful change
from that old party favourite – the sausage roll. Filo pastry is easy to
use and can be readily purchased from most food shops and supermarkets. The pastry,
made into 'purses' can be filled with almost anything you like: vegetables,
spices, various meats and fish or cheeses. Here is one of the more popular suggestions from
the children's parties I have 'hosted'.

INGREDIENTS

8 sheets filo pastry
2 oz (50g) butter

FOR THE FILLING

1 small onion
1 breast or leg of cooked chicken
1 teaspoon ground cumin
1 teaspoon fresh tarragon
   (chopped)
1 dessertspoon mild cheese
8 chives
vegetable oil

METHOD

1. To make the filling, heat a little oil in a small pan. Chop the onion and then fry until soft (about 5 minutes).
2. Dice the chicken into small pieces and add to the pan with the onion and cheese.
3. Now add the cumin and tarragon (chopped) and stir in well. You can add tomatoes or other vegetables at this stage if desired.
4. Leave the mix to cool.
5. Then, preheat your oven to a moderate temperature (B) and carefully unwrap one sheet of the filo pastry.
6. Brush half the sheet with melted butter and fold in half. Brush again with butter and pile some of the filling in the centre.

7. Gather up the edges of the pastry to form a 'purse' and pinch and twist together to seal.

8. Tie a chive around the twisted 'collar', tie a knot, and place carefully onto a greased baking sheet. Repeat to make 30 purses.

9. Brush the purses with a little more butter and bake for about 15 minutes until golden brown.

TIP

Filo pastry is very delicate and can tear easily. Discard any damaged or torn sheets in case the filling leaks out of the purse when cooked. It is nicer when these are served slightly warmed.

WIGGLY WORM CHEESE PASTRIES

Age   1 year upwards
Preparation time   10 minutes
Cooking time   10 minutes
Makes about 50 'worms'

These are really cheese pastries in disguise.
They are delicious and look a lot of fun to eat. If you prefer, you can
follow the same recipe and make them circular or star shaped. You can serve these around
a cheesy or peanut flavoured dip.
(See page 168.)

INGREDIENTS

6 oz (175g) plain flour
4 oz (100g) unsalted butter
3 oz (75g) mild cheese
1 teaspoon mustard powder
1 egg beaten
2 teaspoons sesame seeds
2 teaspoons poppy seeds
salt

METHOD

1. Preheat the oven to a high temperature (C). Mix the flour, salt and mustard powder.
2. Make sure the butter is soft before slicing into small pieces. Combine this with two tablespoons of the beaten egg and mix to a soft dough with the cheese and dry ingredients.
3. Knead the mixture on a floured surface until smooth.
4. Pinch off small pieces of the dough and roll into thin sausage shapes about 4 inches long.
5. Place these on a greased baking sheet and curve into worm shapes.
6. Lightly brush with the remaining egg and sprinkle with the seeds.
7. Bake for 10 minutes until golden brown; cool and serve.

TIP

I always try to serve my party food as I would a meal in my restaurant – that is not too quickly and not all at once. The children seem to enjoy each dish better if they have plenty of time to eat and are not confronted with a large spread from which to choose.

BACON AND SWEETCORN FRITTERS

Age	18 months upwards
Preparation time	10 minutes
Cooking time	20 minutes
Serves	4

These really delicious little 'fritters'
are easy to make and are good served warm as snacks or even used for
adults at drinks parties. That is, in fact, how I discovered that my children enjoyed them;
after I'd eaten most of them and they screamed for more!

INGREDIENTS

4 oz (100g) flour
salt
1 egg
¹/₄ pint (150ml) milk
4 oz (100g) boiled bacon
7¹/₂ oz (215g) can sweetcorn
vegetable oil (enough for deep
*   frying)*
paprika to garnish

METHOD

1. Separate the egg, finely chop the bacon, having first derinded it, and drain the sweetcorn.
2. Having sifted the flour and salt into a bowl, add the egg yolk in a well in the center of the mixture.
3. Beat this gently, slowly adding the milk until all the flour is moistened. Then beat hard for about 2 minutes before leaving the batter to stand in a cool place for about 1 hour.
4. Fold the egg white into the batter and add the bacon and sweetcorn to this mixture.
5. Dip spoonfuls of the mixture into hot, deep oil for 3–4 minutes, until crisp and golden.
6. Drain the 'balls' as they are removed from the oil before serving; be careful that they are not too hot for young children. Garnish with paprika.

TIP

You can replace the bacon with cheese for vegetarian children, or perhaps experiment with mushrooms.

PITTA BREAD POCKETS

Age	1 year upwards
Preparation time	5 minutes
Cooking time	5 minutes
Serves	4

Pitta bread is an excellent way of containing various fillings such as ham, chicken, salads and even sausages. You can buy tiny pitta breads from your local shops. Here is one suggestion.

INGREDIENTS

1 packet cocktail pitta breads
7 oz (200g) tin of tuna (drained)
3 tablespoons mayonnaise
cucumber

METHOD

1. Grill or toast pittas until they are lightly brown.
2. Split them open with a sharp knife.
3. Mix the tuna and mayonnaise and thinly slice the cucumber.
4. Arrange cucumber slices at bottom of pittas and top with the creamy tuna fish. Arrange in a 'fan' around a large plate or dish .

TIP

You can cut pittas into finger shapes, then toast and fan around various dips or even taramasalata, which the children seem to love despite its strong flavour.

Mini Pizzas

Age   1 year upwards
Preparation time   5 minutes
Cooking time   5 minutes
Makes 12 mini pizzas

These aren't true pizzas since
I'm not suggesting making proper pizza dough. For speed, use 2 inch
diameter rounds from bread rolls. Even better, of course, use your home-baked bread. The
main point, however, is the filling. Below is one suggestion, but to be
Italian, you must make up your own toppings.

INGREDIENTS

14 oz (375g) fresh or tinned plum
   tomatoes
1 tablespoon tomato purée
4 oz (100g) Mozzarella cheese
4 oz (100g) ham
2 oz (50g) Cheddar cheese
oregano or fresh basil

METHOD

1. Chop the tomatoes and place in a small saucepan with the tomato purée and a pinch of oregano or fresh basil.
2. Simmer for 5 minutes until thick and spread onto rounds of bread rolls.
3. Top with grated Mozzarella and cheddar cheese and sliced ham. Grill until the topping is bubbling and browned.

TIP

You can use fruit as well as ham, cheese or any other toppings.

EGG HEADS

Age	6 months upwards
Preparation time	10 minutes
Cooking time	15 minutes
Serves	2

The idea here is fairly simple.
You use hard boiled eggs, halved and then stuffed. You can use virtually anything you like and they become egg heads when you arrange the stuffing to look like a face! Here's one way of doing it.

INGREDIENTS

2 hard boiled eggs
4 oz (100g) mushrooms
1 small onion
4 oz (100g) fromage frais

INGREDIENTS FOR GARNISH

1 slice cucumber
1 small tomato
2 leaves of lolla Rosso lettuce
1 small piece of red pepper

METHOD

1. Hard boil the eggs, then cut them in half. Remove the yolks and push them through a sieve.
2. Chop the mushrooms and onion and pan fry until soft. Then purée in your food blender until smooth.
3. Now add the fromage frais and blend in for a few seconds.
4. Fill each halved egg and garnish as follows:
5. Cut the cucumber slice into 8 to achieve thin diamond slices.
6. Peel the tomato and cut into thick slices. Cut each slice into 4 'round noses' with a small party cutter or very sharp knife.
7. Cut the pepper into fine strips to obtain 4 smiles.
8. Finally arrange a little lolla Rosso lettuce at the top of each egg for its hair.

TIP

You can use mayonnaise instead of fromage frais. I tend to use fromage frais and mayonnaise alternately for variation and also because fromage frais is a more healthy food than mayonnaise.

RICE CRISPIE SAVOURIES

Age	1 year upwards
Preparation time	5 minutes
Cooking time	20 minutes
Serves	3

This may first appear to be a funny combination
but it works a treat! They are particularly good for children's parties.

INGREDIENTS

3 oz (75g) plain flour
2 oz (50g) unsalted butter
½ teaspoon mustard powder
1 oz (25g) Cheddar cheese
2 oz (50g) Parmesan cheese
1½ oz (50g) Rice Crispies (or
*   supermarket brand cereal)*
1 egg (beaten)
2 oz (50g) sesame seeds

METHOD

1. Cream together the flour, butter, mustard and grated cheeses.
2. Add the Rice Crispies and shape the dough with your hands into small balls.
3. Dip the balls into the beaten egg, roll in sesame seeds and bake for 20 minutes in a medium preheated oven (B).

TIP

For younger children, I generally leave out the mustard powder or reduce it by half.

MEXICAN DIP

Age	1 year upwards
Preparation time	10 minutes
Cooking time	none
Serves	6–8

INGREDIENTS

1 ripe avocado
3 tablespoons Greek yoghurt
1 tablespoon lemon juice
½ teaspoon paprika
salt and pepper

METHOD

1. Halve and stone the avocado, scoop the flesh into a food processor and add the yoghurt, lemon juice, paprika, salt and pepper. Blend until smooth.
2. Turn the dip into a serving dish and serve with a range of foods such as tortilla chips, cauliflower florets, carrot, celery or cucumber sticks.

DEVIL DOGS

Age	2 years upwards
Preparation time	15 minutes
Cooking time	15 minutes
Serves	4

INGREDIENTS

4 long thin sausages
2 tomatoes
cucumber
1 slice mild Cheddar cheese
4 long granary rolls
cress
tomato sauce (see page 72)

METHOD

1. Cook the sausages under a preheated medium grill, turning frequently, until well cooked. This should take about 15 minutes.
2. Wash the tomatoes and cut each one into 4 wedges. Slice the cucumber and cut two of the slices into quarters. Halve the slice of cheese, then halve each piece again diagonally.
3. Split the rolls in half. Put a sausage in each one and place a piece of cheese on top, to resemble a tongue. Tuck some cress into each end of the rolls.
4. Place the hot dogs on plates and position tomato quarters and cucumber pieces on top of each to resemble eyes. Serve with tomato sauce.

TIP
Use sausages with a high meat content.

ORANGESNAP BASKETS

Age	2 years upwards
Preparation time	20 minutes
Cooking time	12 minutes
Makes 10 baskets	

INGREDIENTS

2 oz (50g) unsalted butter
2 oz (50g) cup castor sugar
3 oz (75g) golden syrup
1 teaspoon orange juice
2 oz (50g) plain flour
1 red-skinned apple
1 orange
2 slices pineapple
4 oz (100g) fresh raspberries
8 oz (225g) fromage frais or Greek
* yoghurt*
sugar to taste

METHOD

1. Place the butter, sugar and syrup into a saucepan. Heat gently until the butter has melted and sugar has dissolved.
2. Remove from the heat and add the orange juice, flour and $\frac{1}{2}$ a teaspoon of grated rind from the orange. Mix together well and then leave to cool.
3. Line 3 baking sheets with non-stick paper and place 4 teaspoonfuls of the mixture, spaced well apart, on each baking sheet.
4. Bake in a preheated oven (B), one sheet at a time, for 10–12 minutes, until the biscuits are spread flat and golden brown.
5. Leave the biscuits on the baking sheets for about 15 seconds, then remove with a palette knife and quickly place each one over an upturned tumbler, ramekin, or even a greased orange. Mould the biscuits carefully with your hands to form basket shapes.

6. Leave to set and then carefully transfer to a wire rack and allow to cool.

7. Core and quarter the apple, peel the orange and cut into segments using a sharp knife, making sure there is no pith. Mix with the apple.

8. Remove the skin and core from the pineapple, then chop the flesh into small cubes. Add to the other fruit with the raspberries.

9. Sweeten the fromage frais or yoghurt with sugar to taste. Fill the baskets with the fruit and top each with a spoonful of fromage frais or yoghurt.

TIP

Keep these snaps in an airtight container and they will last a few days before going soft. You can vary the fruit filling mix to just plain ice-cream for a simpler dish.

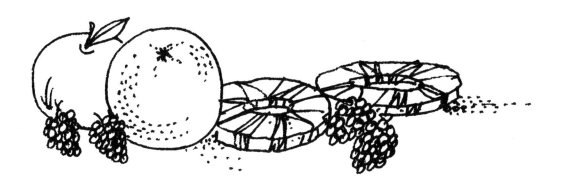

SPACE PEOPLE

Age	1 year upwards
Preparation time	20 minutes
Cooking time	10 minutes
Servings	10

INGREDIENTS

8 oz (225g) plain flour
1 teaspoon mixed spice
1 teaspoon ground ginger
4 oz (100g) cup golden syrup
1½ oz (40g) unsalted butter
3 tablespoons soft brown sugar
1 teaspoon bicarbonate of soda
1 teaspoon water
1 egg yolk
24–28 currants
1 egg white
1 lb (450g) icing sugar
1 tablespoon liquid glucose
1 tablespoon warmed honey
silver balls

METHOD

1. Sift together the flour and spices.
2. Heat the syrup, butter and sugar in a small saucepan. Stir until smooth.
3. Dissolve the bicarbonate of soda in the water. Add to the flour with the melted mixture and the yolk of the egg. Mix this to form a soft dough and knead briefly. Wrap in cling film and leave to rest in the refrigerator for 30 minutes.
4. Evenly roll out the dough and use a gingerbread man cutter to cut out 12–14 men.
5. Place these a little apart, on the baking sheet. Press on currants for eyes. Bake in a medium preheated oven (B) for 6–8 minutes, until lightly browned.
6. Cool on the baking sheet for 5 minutes, then carefully transfer to a wire rack and leave until cooled through.
7. To make the icing, place the egg white and glucose in a bowl and lightly beat together using a fork.

Gradually add the icing sugar and then beat with a wooden spoon until stiff.

8. Add any remaining icing sugar and knead well until a smooth ball is formed. Continue kneading until it is no longer sticky.

9. Use a board well-sprinkled with icing sugar and roll out the icing. Cut out gingerbread men shapes, using the same cutter.

10. Brush the body of each gingerbread biscuit with a little honey. Cut away the head of the icing figures and place the icing sugar 'suits' on the biscuit men.

11. Use any left over icing trimmings to make helmets and attach these with honey. Decorate the suits with silver balls.

TIP

This long method may give you the impression that this recipe represents a lot of work! It's not really, and the end results are worth it.

SCRUMMY SNAILS

Age	2 years upwards
Preparation time	15 minutes
Cooking time	15 minutes
Servings	15

INGREDIENTS

8 oz (225g) self-raising flour
2 oz (50g) unsalted butter
3 oz (75g) Cheddar cheese
7 tablespoons milk
Marmite or Vegemite for spreading
16 cocktail sausages

METHOD

1. Place the flour in a mixing bowl and gradually add small amounts of the butter. Using your fingertips, rub in until the mixture forms a fine crumb consistency.
2. Grate the cheese and stir half into the mixture. Add the milk and mix to a soft dough.
3. Roll out to a rectangle and spread with a very thin layer of Marmite or Vegemite.
4. Sprinkle with the remaining cheese and roll up from a long side, leaving the last 1 inch unrolled. Cut into 15 slices.
5. Lay the slices on a greased baking sheet. Push a sausage into each roll under the unrolled piece of dough, forming the snail's head.
6. Bake in a hot oven (C) for 15 minutes until golden brown. The snails can be served warm or cold.

HEDGEHOGS AND LADYBIRDS

Age	1 year upwards
Preparation time	45 minutes
Cooking time	15 minutes
Servings	12

If you have time, make these delightful treats
for your children's birthday parties. They create a lot of interest and
everyone seems to comment on them!

INGREDIENTS

2 oz (50g) unsalted butter
2 oz (50g) castor sugar
1 egg
2 oz (25g) self-raising flour
1 tablespoon milk
2 oz (50g) plain chocolate
8 oz (225g) icing sugar
4 oz (100g) unsalted butter
1 tablespoon milk
chocolate buttons
silver or gold balls
dolly mixtures
6 oz (125g) bought marzipan
red colouring
milk chocolate

METHOD

1. In a bowl whisk together the butter and sugar until pale and fluffy. Gradually beat in the egg and then fold in the flour and milk.
2. Butter 16 round-base patty tins and divide the mixture into these.
3. Bake in a medium preheated oven (B) for about 15 minutes. When cooked, cool on wire racks.
4. To make the frosting, melt the chocolate and leave to cool. Sift the icing sugar and beat in the butter until the mixture is soft and creamy. Add the melted chocolate and milk.
5. To decorate the hedgehogs; cover half the cold buns with chocolate butter frosting, cut one shape to form a snout. Use halved chocolate buttons with gold balls for the eyes and dolly mixture jellies for the snout.
6. To decorate the ladybirds; colour the marzipan a deep pink with red colouring. Roll this out thinly and use to cover remaining buns. Pipe lines and spots onto the ladybirds with the chocolate butter frosting, use dolly mixtures for the eyes and flakes of milk chocolate for the antennae.

VIKING SHIPS

Age	2 years upwards
Preparation time	15 minutes
Cooking time	none
Serves	6

INGREDIENTS

4 oz (100g) can sardines in oil
4 oz (100g) natural fromage frais
1 tablespoon tomato purée
6 small wholemeal bridge rolls
salt and pepper

INGREDIENTS FOR
DECORATION
radishes
tomatoes
cocktail sticks
parsley sprigs

METHOD

1. Drain the sardines and mash in a bowl. Add the fromage frais, tomato purée and salt and pepper. Mix thoroughly.
2. Halve the rolls and divide the mixture between them, spreading to the edges. Slice the radishes and arrange the slices around the edges like shields.
3. Cut the tomatoes into quarters, then scoop out and discard the centres. Place a cocktail stick in each tomato quarter and attach to the sardine 'boat' to resemble a sail. Attach a small sprig of parsley to each 'sail', to look like a flag.

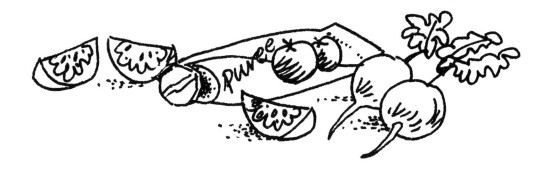

WATERMELON BOATS

Age	9 months upwards
Preparation time	15 minutes
Cooking time	none
Serves	4–6

After all these savoury ideas
it is refreshing to have some novel and tasty sweet ideas. These 'boats'
are arranged on plates and look stunning. Don't suppose they will eat one each though.
The last time I prepared the boats with six children around the table
only two were eaten! Fresh fruit is, of course, a very healthy way to finish off a meal, and
this dish does look exciting as well as refreshing.

INGREDIENTS

4 thin slices of watermelon
3 oranges
2 kiwi fruits
4 sprigs of mint

METHOD

1. Remove all the pips from the watermelon, cut off the skin and lay each slice flat on a plate.
2. Peel and segment the oranges. Arrange as sails, almost like a pyramid, on each of the watermelon slices.
3. Peel and thinly slice the kiwi fruit. Arrange these on a plate under the melon to represent the sea.
4. Finish by putting a fresh mint 'flag' on top of the orange sail.

TIP

Try and serve this dish before the sticky chocolate cakes come out. They will actually eat more of this 'healthy' dish if it is served before the rest of the main food.

KNICKERBOCKER GLORY

Age	1 year upwards
Preparation time	10 minutes
Cooking time	none
Serves	4

This recipe is close to my heart because it was my favourite pudding when I was younger. In fact, if the truth is known, it still is! You can make it out of various fruits, anything in season, or your most favourite. I have made this one with raspberries, strawberries and bananas, but feel free to supplement any of these.

INGREDIENTS

4 oz (100g) fresh raspberries
8 oz (225g) carton of Greek yoghurt or fromage frais
2 bananas
8 oz (225g) strawberries
2 tablespoons clear honey
strawberry or vanilla ice-cream

METHOD

1. Press the raspberries through a sieve to make a purée.
2. Gradually add the yoghurt and the honey and mix until smooth.
3. Place a few of the strawberries and chopped banana in a tall glass and put a spoonful of the delicious yoghurt mix on top.
4. Then put a scoop of ice-cream on top and repeat the layers twice more until you reach the top of the glass.
5. Decorate with some sliced strawberries and serve chilled.

TIP

This is the kind of dish that, although spectacular in itself, can be made even more exciting with a bit of thought. Tall and interesting glasses with the tasteful (and with children, not-too-tasteful) adornment of a few cocktail stirrers always help.

BIRTHDAY CAKE – BASIC SPONGE RECIPE

Age	6 months upwards
Preparation time	15 minutes
Cooking time	30 minutes
Serves	12

You can vary the essence of this classic recipe
by adding flavourings such as orange, lemon, cocoa powder, etc. at stage
2 in the method. Remember to beat thoroughly. You can also use this recipe for square
cakes although you have to adjust the cooking instructions: a little longer
at a slightly lower temperature. The ingredients below will make a 7 inch cake.

INGREDIENTS

6 oz (175g) castor sugar
6 oz (175g) unsalted butter
3 eggs
7 oz (200g) self-raising flour

METHOD

1. In a mixing bowl, cream together the sugar and (soft) butter until it turns a pale colour.
2. Add eggs one at a time with a little sieved flour; then beat thoroughly. Fold in remaining flour with a metal spoon.
3. Pour into two greased and lined 7 inch sandwich tins and bake in a medium preheated oven (B) for 20–30 minutes.
4. Allow the cakes to cool slightly before turning them out onto a wire rack.

TIP

For a bit of fun, when decorating, try using lighted sparklers instead of candles. They are virtually impossible to blow out, but do cause quite a stir when you bring them into a dark room. (Don't use sparklers for very young children.)

10
PICNICS AND PACKED LUNCHES

INTRODUCTION

I remember my packed lunches well. I'm sorry to say Mum, that it was always the same old thing! I know that sounds ungrateful but sandwich spreads, crisps, an apple and a chocolate biscuit, is not my idea of a nutritious and interesting packed lunch. Packed lunches should be varied as often as you vary your children's daily meals. Different types of sandwiches, pittas and perhaps tacos, various fruits (like exotics) all help to make the lunch interesting and exciting. I remember giving my sandwiches away! Please don't let your kids do this – create something more special and they will love to eat it! Picnics should be more varied still and should be highly exciting and imaginative. Good luck!

SANDWICHES – SOME NEW IDEAS

Age	1 year upwards
Preparation time	varied
Cooking time	varied
Serves	various (your choice)

There are two important points about sandwiches.
They do not need to be boring – and children love them. When it comes
to picnic time, remember that the children will probably be especially hungry, so now is
the time to experiment with some new taste combinations and flavours
that the children might not normally be too keen to try. Here are just a few:

1. Chicken liver paté with cucumber and ripe tomatoes
2. Avocado purée with lemon juice and prawns
3. Fromage frais or curd cheese with diced peaches or apple
4. Mashed banana with fromage frais
5. Taramasalata with cocktail pitta breads
6. Kipper paté with tomatoes and dill
7. Coleslaw with grated cheese
8. Peanut butter (smooth) with seedless grapes
9. Soft cream cheese with pineapple
10. Hard boiled eggs mashed with mayonnaise and Marmite
11. Pasta with grated cheese, chives and mushrooms (cooked with a little garlic)
12. Tuna fish mixed with diced peppers, cucumber, sweetcorn and mayonnaise
13. Cream cheese with fresh strawberries
14. Thinly sliced cucumber (marinated in wine vinegar) and served with salad cream and dill
15. Marmite with chopped tomatoes and fresh basil
16. Cream cheese, pineapple and sesame seeds
17. Cottage cheese in a bagel with avocado and lemon juice
18. Taramasalata and chives
19. Chicken livers mashed with fried onions and hard boiled eggs

20. Turkey with coleslaw
21. Grated cheese mixed with grated carrot and onion
22. Cottage cheese with grated apples and chopped tomatoes
23. Turkey with cranberry sauce
24. Cottage cheese and banana
25. Fruit curd
26. Hummus
27. Tuna with mayonnaise and a little curry powder
28. Cottage cheese with chives and sultanas
29. Tomato and red pepper
30. Cream cheese with dates and banana

TIP

Of course, the fillings need not be the only thing that varies. Try a variety of breads, rolls and even muffins.

KIPPER PATÉ

Age	1 year upwards
Preparation time	10 minutes
Cooking time	5 minutes
Serves	4

This is a very simple and tasty recipe,
delicious for all the family. You will need to keep this quite cold when
out on a picnic.

INGREDIENTS

1 kipper (undyed)
2 tomatoes
2 oz (50g) unsalted butter
small bunch of chives

METHOD

1. Steam or poach the kipper in a little water, in a covered saucepan, for 5 minutes.
2. Remove this from the pan and allow to cool. When cool, remove all the bones from the kipper.
3. Skin, deseed and finely chop the tomatoes.
4. Blend together the kipper, tomatoes and (chopped) chives with the melted butter.
5. Refrigerate and serve cold.

TIP

It is easier to remove the bones when you steam or poach the kipper. Alternatively, you can blend the kipper, hence mashing the bones to a purée or pulp through a fine nylon sieve.

CHICKEN LIVER PATÉ

Age	1 year upwards
Preparation time	10 minutes
Cooking time	10 minutes
Serves	6

This is a soft, creamy paté,
again easy to make and keep – it will readily store in the refrigerator
for two or three days. This, and other patés, can be taken out on the picnic in a separate
container or can be put in sandwiches first.

INGREDIENTS

8 oz (225g) chicken livers
1 medium onion
2 large sprigs of parsley
3 tablespoons of freshly squeezed
    orange juice
1 dessertspoon of lemon juice
1 clove garlic
vegetable or olive oil

METHOD

1. Chop the parsley and place in a mixing bowl with the livers. Pour the orange juice over them.
2. Finely chop the onion and crush the garlic. In a thick-bottomed frying pan, fry them in the oil until soft. Then, add the livers and lemon juice.
3. Cook for about 10 minutes so that the livers are still just a little pink in the centre; drain off and reserve the cooking liquor.
4. Blend the livers in a processor with half the reserved liquor and the parsley until smooth.
5. Refrigerate so that the paté sets and serve cold.

TIP

Do not overcook the livers when frying or they will become tough, dry and rather bitter, and at the same time, do not undercook them!

CATHERINE WHEEL SANDWICHES

Age	6 months upwards
Preparation time	15 minutes
Cooking time	none

Makes about 28 'wheels'

These little 'wheel' sandwiches are ideal
for younger children on picnics – and also perfect for parties. They make
a nice change from ordinary sandwiches and usually get eaten first!

INGREDIENTS

3 oz (75g) cottage cheese
2 tablespoons chives
1 tomato
4 slices brown bread
a handful of sultanas

METHOD

1. Skin and chop the tomato. Mix this with the cheese and chives until smooth, then stir in the sultanas.
2. Remove the crusts of the bread and roll out with a rolling pin, so that each slice is long and fairly thin.
3. Spread the cheese and sultana mix onto the bread and roll up firmly like a Swiss roll.
4. Wrap each roll with clingfilm to keep fresh.
5. Cut each roll into about 7 slices.

TIP

Do not roll the bread out too finely or it will tear, but if it is too thick it will not roll up tightly enough. Believe me, it is worth the effort!

SERENA'S CARROT SALAD

Age   6 months upwards
Preparation time   5 minutes
Cooking time   none
Serves   4

Serena, luckily, isn't a fussy eater although
she does dislike salads except for this one! It seems to go with anything.

INGREDIENTS

1 lb (450g) of carrots
1 small bunch chives
^{1}/$_2$ teaspoon of Dijon mustard (or
    similar)
1 tablespoon wine vinegar
5 oz (140g) sultanas
3 tablespoons olive oil
pinch of salt

METHOD

1. Peel and finely grate the carrots.
2. Place all ingredients in a bowl and toss until carrots
   are well coated.
3. Leave in marinade in the fridge, ideally for a few
   hours.

TIP

You can eat this with a teaspoon on its own, spread on fingers of bread or eat with other
picnic items. It is very refreshing and healthy.

CHEESY PASTIES

Age	3 years upwards
Preparation time	35 minutes
Cooking time	20 minutes
Serves	6

A useful recipe for good homemade pasties.
Again, fillings can vary as much as you like. Whatever the choice of filling,
they do make particularly good picnic food.

INGREDIENTS

2 tablespoons oil
1 onion
2 celery sticks
1 clove garlic
1 tablespoon plain wholemeal flour
3 fl oz (75ml) milk
3 oz (75g) Edam cheese
3 oz (75g) sweetcorn kernels
fresh parsley (chopped)
1 teaspoon Dijon mustard
12 oz (325g) frozen wholemeal
*   puff pastry*
2 teaspoons sesame seeds
salt and pepper

METHOD

1. Chop the onion and celery and crush the garlic. Fry gently in the oil until softened.
2. Stir in the flour, then gradually blend in the milk. Bring to the boil, stirring constantly, and cook for 3 minutes until thickened.
3. Finely chop the parsley and stir into the mixture with the cheese, sweetcorn, mustard and salt and pepper. Leave to cool.
4. On a well floured surface roll out the pastry and cut into eight 6 inch rounds.
5. Divide the mixture between the rounds, mounding it in the centre. Moisten the edge with water, fold in half to make a semi-circle and pinch the edges firmly together.
6. Place on a baking sheet, brush with water and sprinkle with sesame seeds. Make a hole in each one.
7. Bake in a high preheated oven (C) for 20 minutes. Leave to cool on the baking sheet.

TIP

The pasties can be individually wrapped and frozen before the baking stage only, not after. Great to use for a snack, picnics or packed lunch treat.

PICNIC SQUARES

Age   5 years upwards
Preparation time   10 minutes
Cooking time   25–30 minutes
Makes 24 squares

These are certainly as good to eat
as a bought crunchy snack, and definitely a lot healthier for your children.

INGREDIENTS

3 tablespoons malt extract
2 tablespoons clear honey
4 fl oz (100ml) sunflower oil
8 oz (225g) oats
1 oz (25g) sunflower seeds
1 oz (25g) peanuts

METHOD

1. Gently heat the malt, honey and oil in a pan until mixed well. Remove from the heat.
2. Finely chop or crush the peanuts and add together with the remaining ingredients. Mix thoroughly.
3. Press into a greased 12 × 8 inch Swiss-roll tin and smooth the top with a palette knife.
4. Bake in a medium preheated oven (B) for 25–30 minutes.
5. Cool in the tin for 2 minutes, then cut into squares.
6. Leave to cool through completely before removing from the tin.

SARDINE TART

Age	3 years upwards
Preparation time	35 minutes
Cooking time	45 minutes
Serves	4–6

INGREDIENTS

6 oz (175g) flour
1½ oz (40g) unsalted butter
1½ oz (40g) lard
3 tablespoons chilled water
2 oz (50g) can sardines in oil
1 small onion
juice of 1 lemon
2½ oz (65g) natural yoghurt
2½ fl oz (120ml) fresh single cream
2 oz (50g) cottage cheese
2 eggs
salt and freshly ground pepper
fresh parsley

METHOD

1. To make the pastry cut the butter and lard into small pieces. Rub into the flour and pinch of salt using the fingertips until the mixture resembles fine bread-crumbs. Mix in the water using a round-bladed knife.
2. Once the mixture has formed a dough, knead gently for a few seconds. Rest the pastry for 30 minutes in the fridge.
3. Roll out the pastry and use to line a 7 inch flan ring.
4. Finely chop the onion and, using the oil from the sardines, fry until soft. Place on the base of the flan case and sprinkle with half the lemon juice.
5. Beat together the yoghurt, fresh cream, cottage cheese, eggs and seasoning. Pour this over the onions and arrange the sardines on top like the spokes of a wheel. Sprinkle with the remaining lemon juice and freshly ground pepper.
6. Bake in a high oven (C) for 15 minutes then reduce the temperature for the final 25 minutes.
7. Garnish with fresh parsley. This dish can be served hot or cold.

TIP

If you can get them, try this recipe with fresh sardines – it improves the flavour no end.

CORNISH PASTIES

Age	3 years upwards
Preparation time	30 minutes
Cooking time	45 minutes
Serves	4

This is a good, old traditional pasty recipe.
You can make a vegetarian version of this dish by omitting the beef and
adding a greater variety of vegetables.

INGREDIENTS

8 oz (225g) flour
2 oz (50g) unsalted butter
2 oz (50g) lard
2 tablespoons chilled water
pinch of salt
6 oz (175g) stewing beef
2 potatoes
1 small turnip
1 onion
salt and freshly ground pepper
1 egg to glaze

METHOD

1. To make the pastry cut the butter and lard into small pieces. Rub into the flour and a pinch of salt using the fingertips until the mixture resembles fine bread-crumbs. Mix in the water using a round-bladed knife.
2. Once the mixture has formed a dough, knead gently for a few seconds. Place the pastry in the fridge for 30 minutes.
3. Roll out the pastry and, using a saucer as a guide, cut into four circles.
4. Trim any excess fat from the beef and cut the meat into paper-thin slices with a sharp knife.
5. Peel and coarsely grate the potatoes and turnip. Finely chop the onion. Mix the vegetables with the meat.

6. Pile the filling in the centre of each pastry circle. Season with salt and freshly ground pepper and top with a knob of butter.

7. Dampen the pastry edges with cold water and carefully draw up two edges to meet on top of the filling. Pinch and twist the pastry firmly together to form a neat fluted and curved pattern. Cut a small air vent in the side of each.

8. Beat the egg and lightly brush this over the top. Place on a buttered baking tray.

9. Bake in a high preheated oven (C) for 10 minutes. Then reduce the heat slightly and bake for a further 30 minutes.

SCOTTISH CHEESEMEATS

Age	3 years upwards
Preparation time	20 minutes
Cooking time	10 minutes
Makes 12 cheesemeats	

INGREDIENTS

4 oz (100g) English Cheddar cheese
1 lb (450g) sausagemeat
1 tablespoon French mustard
salt and freshly ground pepper
flour
1 egg
1 oz (25g) dry breadcrumbs

METHOD

1. Divide the cheese into 12 even-sized pieces.
2. Blend the sausagemeat with the mustard and season with salt and black pepper. This is best done in a food processor to make sure the blending is even.
3. Roll each piece of cheese in sausagemeat, making sure the cheese is completely encased and forming medium-sized balls.
4. Beat the egg and then roll the balls lightly in flour, beaten egg and breadcrumbs, making sure they are well coated and pressing the crumbs on well.
5. Chill for 30 minutes to set the crumbs, then deep fry until golden brown.
6. Drain well on kitchen paper. Serve cold.

WHOLEMEAL TOMATO QUICHE

Age	1 year upwards
Preparation time	20 minutes
Cooking time	45 minutes
Serves	8

A good vegetarian recipe using wholemeal flour
for a change. It also uses yoghurt and less cream as a healthier version.

INGREDIENTS

4 oz (100g) plain flour
4 oz (100g) wholemeal flour
5 oz (140g) unsalted butter
4 oz (100g) spring onions
8 small firm tomatoes
2 eggs
5 oz (140g) natural yoghurt
3 tablespoons fresh single cream
1 teaspoon dried tarragon
salt and freshly ground pepper

METHOD

1. Mix both types of flour together and using your fingertips, rub in 4 oz of the butter. Add 4 tablespoons of water and blend to a firm dough. The mixture should line a large flan dish or eight 4 inch individual Yorkshire pudding tins. Bake blind in the oven (C) for about 15 minutes.
2. Trim and snip the spring onions and fry in the remaining butter until golden brown.
3. Skin the tomatoes and cut into thin slices; arrange them in overlapping circles in the pastry. Scatter the spring onions over the top.
4. Whisk the eggs with the yoghurt, fresh cream, tarragon, cooked spring onions and seasoning, and spoon carefully into the pastry.
5. Bake in a medium oven (B) for 20–25 minutes until just set. Serve warm.

TIP

These are especially tasty served warm as a main dish – perhaps with a cream or tomato sauce.

APPLE CAKE

Age	1 year upwards
Preparation time	15 minutes
Cooking time	1 hour 45 minutes
Serves	6–8

You've probably tried apple pie,
but have you had apple cake? Delicious served warm with custard sauce
(page 164) or with cream or fromage frais. If you are giving this dessert to very young
children try to avoid using cream.

INGREDIENTS

8 oz (225g) cooking apples
8 oz (225g) sultanas
¼ pint (150ml) milk
6 oz (175g) soft brown sugar
12 oz (325g) self-raising flour
2 level teaspoons mixed spice
6 oz (175g) unsalted butter
1 egg
1 oz (25g) demerara sugar

METHOD

1. Peel, core and chop the apples and mix together with the sultanas, milk and sugar.
2. Sieve together the flour and spice, then mix with the butter.
3. Beat the egg and add to the fruit mixture. Mix well with the flour, spice and butter.
4. Place mixture in a buttered and lined 8 inch square cake tin. Sprinkle with demerara sugar and bake in a medium preheated (B) oven for 1¾ hours, until risen and golden brown.

STUFFED TOMATOES WITH TUNA

Age	1 year upwards
Preparation time	15 minutes
Cooking time	15 minutes
Serves	4

You can use stuffed tomatoes filled
with many different fillings as picnic or packed-lunch fillers. Cherry tomatoes
make great one mouthful morsels which I find tastier and less messy.

INGREDIENTS

3 oz (75g) tuna fresh (or tinned)
1 egg
1 tablespoon chives chopped
1 tablespoon mayonnaise or
    fromage frais
4 tomatoes

METHOD

1. Hard boil the egg.
2. Boil some water and blanch the tomatoes for 1 minute till skins start to peel off.
3. Remove from water, skin, and slice off top.
4. Scoop out seeds and when the egg is done, mash it with the tuna, mayonnaise or fromage frais and chives, and stuff each tomato. Replace tops.

TIP

Do not over-blanch the tomatoes or they will collapse. You may find 1 minute is too long
for tiny cherry tomatoes – keep an eye on them!

RICE CRISPIE BALLS

Age   2 years upwards
Preparation time   10 minutes
Cooking time   15 minutes
Makes about 12 balls

I love them! But then I seem to love
most of the fresh party foods I prepare for my girls.

INGREDIENTS

3 oz (75g) plain flour
2 oz (50g) unsalted butter
¼ teaspoon English mustard
1 oz (25g) grated Cheddar cheese
2 oz (50g) Rice Crispies
1 egg beaten
2 oz (50g) sesame seeds

METHOD

1. Cream together the flour, butter and cheese and add
   mustard.
2. Add the Rice Crispies and shape the dough into balls
   with your hands.
3. Dip each ball into beaten egg then sesame seeds and
   bake in a hot oven for 15 minutes till golden brown.

TIP

You can make these sweet by adding honey instead of mustard and a grated fruit instead of
cheese if you prefer.

FAST FOOD PIZZAS

Age	1 year upwards
Preparation time	15 minutes
Cooking time	10 minutes
Serves	2

Homemade pizzas taste the best!
What is even better is that they are very easy to make. Follow these
instructions.

INGREDIENTS

1 spring onion (finely chopped)
2 tomatoes (skinned and chopped)
4 button mushrooms (sliced)
1 dessertspoon tomato purée
1 teaspoon fresh basil (chopped)
1½ oz (40g) Mozzarella cheese
¼ French bread stick
2 oz (50g) unsalted butter

METHOD

1. Fry the onions, tomatoes and mushrooms in the butter till soft (2–3 minutes) and stir in tomato purée.
2. Cut the bread in half and spread the tomato mix over.
3. Put the chopped basil on top followed by slices of Mozzarella cheese.
4. Grill (under hot grill) for 3–4 minutes till golden.

TIP

You can vary this enormously by adding pineapple, ham, chicken, tuna or whatever to the tomato mix before spreading onto the bread.

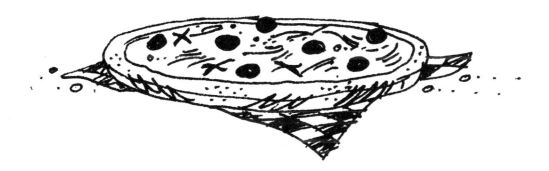